A Dream Come True

OLIVIA TUFFIN

For Rosie

First published in the UK in 2018 by Nosy Crow Ltd
The Crow's Nest, 14 Baden Place
Crosby Row, London SE1 1YW
www.nosycrow.com

ISBN: 978 1 78800 0536

A CIP catalogue record for this book is available from the British Library.

Printed and bound in Great Britain by Clays Ltd, Elcograf S.p.A.
Typeset by Tiger Media

Papers used by Nosy Crow are made from wood grown in
sustainable forests.

1 3 5 7 9 8 6 4 2

PROLOGUE

The girl placed a protective hand on the pony's neck as the men talked in low voices a few steps away. There were always meetings, conversations in corners, hushed voices. She ignored most of it. It was business, he said, nothing to do with the ponies. But she couldn't ignore this.

We can get another rider if we need to… The words echoed in her ears, the meaning clear. She was disposable. He owned the pony, he controlled what the two of them did together, where they jumped, how high. What had started as a dream was now a nightmare. She knew the pony was being pushed too soon but she didn't dare speak up. There were rumours, of course. Everyone had heard them. About the girl and the pony that had gone before her.

Sighing, she leaned into the pony, closing her eyes as she let his conker-and-white mane brush over her cheeks. She'd read an article recently about the other competitors in her big class, other pony club members. She'd studied their delighted smiles in the photos as they collected their qualifier's rosette: a boy on a lovely bay, a girl on a chestnut, another girl on the sweetest roan pony with the cheekiest face. All so happy, all so free. *If he was my very own pony…* she thought wistfully for the hundredth time. But he wasn't,

and she would do all she could to keep riding him. And if that meant staying silent when everything felt wrong, then she had no choice. He was all she had.

Chapter 1

Pulling the elaborate rosette down from the display in the kitchen, Alice Smalley let the silken tails run through her fingers. It transported her back to the moment the red rosette had been pinned to Secret's bridle, almost eclipsing his whole face! He'd stood so proudly, lapping up the attention. Alice could still hear the ring of applause in her ears, and she bathed in the wonderful memory of the lap of honour on the green, springy turf of the South of England showjumping arena. Of course, Secret had tried to eat one of the fabulous flower displays while the prizes were handed out, but that had only seemed to make the crowd love the cheeky red gelding even more.

Closing her eyes for a minute, Alice took a deep breath. The warm sunshine and bright summer days spent hacking out and attending pony club lessons had given way to swirling leaves, frosty mornings and muddy New Zealand rugs as winter closed in. It all meant Olympia, and Alice's class, the Pony Club Christmas Tree Stakes, was just around the corner.

Crossing out another day on the calendar, Alice studied it for a moment. The time between now and the Christmas show seemed impossibly short all of a sudden.

Alice had been to Olympia before with her

mum's ponies, including showing the late, great Lachlan in the Mountain and Moorland show class, but she couldn't wait to jump there on her very own pony, a pony *she'd* trained. Secret.

Alice had owned the cheeky gelding since he was just six months old. He had been destined for the show ring, like her mum's other ponies. But despite his impeccable looks and movement, Secret *really* hadn't been cut out for showing. His – and Alice's – great love was showjumping, and it had taken a while for Alice to convince her mum they should switch paths. But Secret had come further than anyone had thought possible, and Alice had even started to believe they might have a real future.

She turned to the photos of her showjumping heroes, the Whitakers, Nick Skelton and top girl showjumper Devon Jenkins, who was a nation-wide pony club heroine. Alice hoped she'd meet some of them at Olympia, maybe even get an autograph or two! Deep in thought, she jumped as the stable door of the kitchen swung open and a blast of icy air brought in a familiar face, one Alice hadn't seen in a while. It was her friend Finn, cowboy boots as ever on his feet and a big smile on his face. Alice's tummy instantly flipped upside down.

"Hi, stranger!" Crossing the room, Alice hugged him. She hadn't expected to see him until she got to London. Finn had been training with a famous pony stunt team, the Rebel Riders, who were in England for Olympia and had asked Finn to join them. Finn, who disliked school, had even been pulled out of his studies to home school while he concentrated on the training. But because of this, Alice had barely seen him since the end of the summer, since that amazing day at the pony club championships. But they'd kept in touch with phone calls that lasted for hours, Alice filling him in on life at home, Secret's latest escapades, and Finn telling Alice how his training was going.

"Hey." Finn smiled, looking down at the huge rosette still clutched in Alice's hand. "So close now!"

"I know," Alice said with a gulp. "Come and see Secret!" And taking Finn's hand she practically dragged him out into the yard. The light was fading, and the ponies looked out from their stable doors with hopeful interest as they waited for their evening feeds. A sharp bang on the door told them where Secret was! He would bang his stable door as soon as he saw a light go on in the house in the mornings, making sure no one slept in, much to the annoyance of Alice's mum and dad. Adding a shrill whinny to his bangs, his delight at seeing his two favourite people only too clear, Secret nodded his head up and down. He'd been out in the field all day, a special hood and rug on to keep his coat – newly clipped for Olympia – sleek and shiny.

"Hello, boy," Finn said warmly, reaching up to stroke Secret. Alice knew Finn had a huge amount of affection for her pony. It had been partly because of Secret that Finn was now so closely involved with the Rebel Riders, the pony stunt team from Spain. After a chance meeting with a fashion magazine team in France, Alice had suggested Finn's family home, Rookham Manor, as a possible shoot location and this had saved the family from financial ruin. The Rebel Riders had taken part in the photo shoot and after that, Celia, the head of the stunt team, had taken Finn under her wing and asked him to join the riders at Olympia.

Actually, Alice thought with a smile, it was because of Secret that she and Finn were even friends in the first place! Secret had thrown Alice at his very first ridden show and bolted out across a fairground, and Finn had caught him. Alice and Secret had come so far since that day, and she knew Finn was very proud of them both. *She* was proud of them both, but it was all going to be put to the test soon, at Olympia, in front of thousands of people. She shivered, and Finn turned to her, as if reading her thoughts.

"Come on then," he grinned. "Let's see you ride!"

★

A short while later and Alice was mounted on Secret, pulling her coat up higher around her neck. The cold air was heavy with the tang of woodsmoke, and Secret's breath was like a dragon's plume as they halted next to Finn, who was perched on a jump pole in the centre of the arena. Secret's rich red mane was now a contrast to the creamy pink of his clipped coat. Alice missed his fluffy coat and burying her hands into the warmth of his woolly neck, but she knew clipped was better for Secret with their rigorous training schedule and jumping under the hot, bright lights of Olympia. Once they were home from the big show, Secret was going to have a good rest and be allowed to get as hairy and muddy as he liked!

"He's looking the best I've ever seen," Finn said admiringly. "Dad was saying how hard you've worked."

"Thanks." Alice glowed with pride. Secret had matured into a gorgeous-looking pony. He'd always been handsome, but the gangly baby stage was long behind him now and he was strong and well muscled. His elegant head and curved neck added class.

It was only a year ago that Alice had started her training with Angus, Finn's dad, when he took over the junior showjumping team at Hilltops pony club. They'd got off to a tough start! Secret had unlimited talent and Alice had had to adapt to his bounding enthusiasm. But as the year progressed they'd started to make a name for themselves locally, doing well on the circuit, before landing second place and highest-placed UK rider at the prestigious Festival of the Horse in France. It had been during that class that Secret had been talent-spotted and invited to try out for the Olympia qualifiers.

From that moment on it had been a whirlwind summer as Alice had trained and prepared Secret alongside helping her mum ride the yard ponies at the big county shows. It had meant the world to Alice when Finn had come down to the pony club summer championships from the Midlands, where the Flying Fillies, his family's pony display team, were giving a demo, just so he could support

Alice and Secret on their big day. She smiled, reliving the moment she'd won the class. Someone had once said qualifying for Olympia was almost more exciting than the event itself, but Alice was still off-the-scale excited about the next couple of weeks!

Chapter 2

"So what's the plan?" Finn asked, once Alice had popped over the grid and slowed Secret to a springy trot.

"Just as your dad said," she called breathlessly. Secret's jumping power still caught her by surprise. "A couple more jumping sessions and then just hacking until the day itself."

"Sounds great," Finn nodded.

"Are *you* all set?" Alice asked him as they headed back up to the yard. Angus had advised her to keep schooling sessions short and sweet, and the little Welsh still felt fresh as he jogged back to the stables, where the yard lights were throwing orange shadows over the cobbles in the dusk. It was early December but it already felt really Christmassy, and fairy lights – Alice's yearly tradition – twinkled in the trees next to the gate.

She had a busy evening ahead. Fergus, her mum's head groom, was taking a long-overdue holiday to see his family in Scotland, and it meant Alice was helping her mum more than ever. It was relentless and hard work, but Alice was at her happiest out in the yard, and she knew her mum was grateful. Josephine took in ponies for clients to school and take to shows, and although December was a quiet month, they still had plenty of ponies to look after.

"Yep," Finn nodded. "I think so. Horatio and I head off to London tomorrow."

Horatio was Finn's own pony, a gorgeous snowy-white Highland with a thick mane and a wise face. He'd been close to being put down due to his dangerous behaviour before Angus had saved him and rehabilitated him. He'd gone with Finn to train and had done so well, he was even going to join the Olympia team ponies.

"It's amazing, isn't it?" Alice paused as she fastened Secret's stable rug after untacking him. "How France changed everything so much. First my Olympia qualifier, and your chance to ride with the Rebel Riders."

"I know," Finn smiled. "And Secret had a good part to play as well!"

"How's Sasha with it all?" Alice asked.

Sasha was Finn's older sister. She and Finn had continued with the Flying Fillies after their mum's death and made a real triumph of it, despite lots of trials along the way. After the success of the photo shoot, Angus had had regular bookings for the yard and the fees ensured they could keep their ponies. But Alice knew that riding with the Rebel Riders had given Finn a taste of something different, and perhaps life beyond home.

"Sash is fine," he said. "Actually, I meant to tell you. She's just been offered a job working with young horses in the Middle East. It's a six-month gig, a bit longer if she wants. I think she's going to take it. If I'm riding with Celia and the Rebel Riders then we don't need to advertise the Flying Fillies and the ponies can stay at home."

"Oh, wow," Alice said, thinking of Sasha, who was just as fearless on a horse as Finn. "That's big news!"

Finn nodded. "Yep," he replied. "It's a huge opportunity, and I know she was wanting to leave home at some point. I hope she'll be back…" He hesitated. "Still, I guess everything changes at some point."

Then he glanced at his watch and gave Alice an apologetic look.

"Sorry, Al," he said. "I need to get the bus home. I've got loads to do before I go back to training."

"It's no problem," Alice replied. She secretly thought how amazing it was that Finn had bothered to come all the way over just to check in with her and see Secret. She knew he was living a totally different life to her right now. Alice was at school for a couple more weeks, and Finn would soon be in London with the Rebel Riders.

"I'll see you soon?" Alice asked, a little shyly.

"Of course," Finn grinned. "Two weeks is nothing. See you, Al. In the big city!"

And then with one final hug he was gone. Alice watched him go, her feelings mixed, before she drew herself up straight. Two weeks, that was all that was left now! It was no time at all. And the most important thing of all was Secret.

Later, Alice reflected on Finn's earlier words as she skipped Secret's stable out. *Everything changes at some point*. What would change for her and her mischievous, loyal red pony?

★

Since the death of her beloved pony, Lachlan, at the start of the year, Alice's mum had stepped back a little from showing. The sweet Highland pony had been killed in an accident on a snow-covered road, saving the life of both Alice's mum, and Ella, another pony, and it had been devastating for the whole yard.

Despite this, they still qualified two ponies for the Horse of the Year Show, including Archie, the pony Finn regularly rode. This year, unlike before, Finn actually rode at the big show, earning second place and firmly cementing him in Josephine's good books. She'd taken a while to come round to Finn, and it had been even harder when it had come to light that Finn's dad and Josephine had a rocky history involving an injured pony. But since then, Josephine had taken on Ella, a little grey mare, the pony Lachlan had saved. Finn and Angus had originally rescued her from Spain, and she had been instrumental in binding the two families together. She could now be ridden, and Alice's mum enjoyed long meandering hacks over the downs with Alice on Secret, and dressage lessons, which they both adored.

Today they were all going to take part in a prelim dressage test at Hilltops, the local equestrian centre where Alice had spent a lot of time training with the pony club.

"Alice!"

A familiar voice welcomed Alice as she pushed open the door to Hilltops' café. Her mum was warming Ella up in the outdoor school and Alice had headed in to get a warm drink to thaw out her frozen hands. There was still fifteen minutes until Ella's class, enough time for a quick catch-up with her pony club friends.

"Hey, Amy," Alice smiled. Amy had been one of the first people to welcome her into the pony club branch, and they'd remained friends. Although Amy was also good friends with Hannah, whose dad owned the centre. Hannah and Alice's relationship was fragile at best, but at least they could be polite and civil now.

"Is that your mum's Spanish pony?" Amy linked arms with Alice as she headed to the counter.

Alice nodded. "Yep," she replied. "They're doing great, aren't they?"

"I'll say," Amy said in an admiring voice. Then

she changed the subject, her eyes sparkling. "How's it going?"

She didn't even have to name the event. Olympia now consumed Alice's every thought, every minute that ticked by taking her closer to the huge international arena. She wasn't scared yet, but her excitement bordered on a slight hysteria that mingled with nerves. The kind of nerves that meant eating could be difficult if she thought too much about it, and her dreams were occupied by huge showjumps. But she was trying to go with it. Angus had told her that nerves were a good thing, that they would keep her focused and sharp. She hoped so!

"Have you heard June's organised a bus?" Amy continued with a grin, and Alice blinked at her. June was the district commissioner of the Hilltops branch.

"A what?" she frowned, and Amy chuckled.

"A bus! And it's fully booked!" she said. "The whole branch is coming to London to cheer you on!" Seeing Alice's face as she swallowed hard, Amy nudged her. "Hey," she said kindly. "We're all so proud. No one from Hilltops has qualified for Olympia before!"

"Thanks," Alice said nervously. "Pile on the pressure more, why don't you!" But she couldn't help feel a certain amount of pride as well.

"Do you know any of the other riders?" Amy continued, and Alice shook her head.

"No," she said. "It's all new to me."

"Well, I know for a fact Leah Edwards is in your class!" Amy said, and Alice looked at her blankly. The name rang a bell. "Leah's the one who's riding for Hadley Feeds," Amy continued. "On that amazing pony Kite B? She was in *Pony* mag last month, did you see? A massive feature."

Suddenly Alice remembered. "Oh, yes!" she

said. "I did read about her." She gulped. "She's going to be tough competition!"

Leah Edwards was a bit of a hero among the pony club. She'd had a job working at a riding stables before being star-spotted at a show and offered a huge sponsorship deal, including the chance to ride an amazing pony who had been imported from the Netherlands. Alice knew she was very lucky owning her own pony, especially one like Secret, but she couldn't help but feel slightly envious of Leah. Sponsorship had to mean you were worth investing in. Leah must be seriously good, and Alice wondered if there was any way she might get to talk to her, to get some tips. Now she and Secret had had a taste of the big arenas, she wanted to get as far as she could!

Then, glancing at her watch, she realised her mum was going into the arena in just a couple of minutes. Grabbing her hot chocolate, she gave

Amy a quick hug.

"Good luck if I don't see you before Olympia!" Amy grinned. "You'll know where the Hilltops branch are sitting – we'll be cheering the loudest!"

And Alice didn't doubt it. Joining the local pony club branch really had been the best decision ever!

Chapter 3

Ella excelled herself. Although Alice's mum had trained countless ponies over the years, qualifying many of them for the big shows such as Horse of the Year and indeed Olympia, the pride on her face as she rode Ella out of the arena on a loose rein made Alice feel a bit teary. Ella was very special to her mum. She had taken over the mare's care after it was clear to everyone they'd struck up a strong bond, and since then Ella had flourished. It might have only been a prelim test, but it was far, far more than anyone ever thought she'd be capable of. When she'd first arrived at Park Farm, she'd been too nervous to even set foot out of her stable, but Secret had helped with that. In fact, Alice mused, her little red gelding had opened so many doors, for people and ponies alike!

"Fantastic, Josie!"

A familiar voice made both Alice and her mum turn and smile, and Ella whicker in recognition. It was Angus, Finn's dad. He was the resident pony club instructor and was often at Hilltops giving lessons.

"I always knew she was something special," Angus continued admiringly. "Her movement is incredible. She could go really far!"

"I'll aim her for a novice test," Alice's mum

smiled. "But in all honesty, I've no real ambitions, other than to enjoy her. Anyway, it's all about Alice and Secret for now!"

"Of course," Angus chuckled. "Still on for our lesson tomorrow?"

"You bet!" Alice grinned. Then she hesitated, feeling a little shy. "How was Finn when you dropped him and Horatio back in London?"

"Oh, so excited," Angus said. "Doubt I'll hear a peep from him, unless I nag him!"

Alice smiled, realising she hadn't even checked her phone to see if Finn had been in contact. She was so busy thinking about Olympia and helping her mum, she hadn't had time to worry about anything else. She was once again struck by the different paths their lives were taking, and suddenly she realised that was OK. She'd see him soon enough.

★

Finn might not have been great at contacting his dad, but he did text Alice the very next morning to find out how Ella had got on. Alice was in the middle of filling hay nets and scrabbled for her phone as she heard the ping, unable to stop the smile as she opened the message.

Hey, she read. *How did Ella get on? Hope Secret is good today in your lesson. Really busy here, but fun. We went on the London Eye after training last night! Amazing X*

Alice tried to imagine Finn in London, in the bustling crowds, on the London Eye, and failed. She only really ever imagined him in the meadows at Rookham, riding bareback on Horatio. She smiled. There he was doing amazing things and she was here, covered in hay and mud from where she'd had to wrestle Secret's filthy New Zealand rug off earlier.

Ella did brilliantly, she replied. *Saw your dad, he*

was really pleased. Looking forward to later, I'll let you know how Secret goes. What was the London Eye like? Was it scary? X

Finn didn't reply until later when Alice was filling the last of the water buckets for sweet, bossy Porridge, her mum's black Shetland.

No, it was ace. You'd have loved it! X

And Alice smiled to think of her friend having such an amazing time in London.

★

"OK, Alice!"

Angus pulled his collar up a little tighter, keeping off the frigid chill of the indoor arena at Hilltops. Alice barely noticed the cold once she started to warm Secret up. The adrenalin of jumping him, coupled with how hard she had to concentrate on not letting him bound over the poles, meant her cheeks were quickly flushed and layers were discarded on the arena fence. She turned Secret to face her instructor.

"So," Angus reached up to give Secret a stroke, "are you happy with everything?"

Alice nodded. "Jump today, and once more next week and then just hack." She repeated what she and Angus had discussed a few times. "And then jump in the warm-up at Olympia, but don't overdo it."

"Exactly." Angus nodded. "So let's have a good session today." He gestured to the short course he'd set up. "Time to jump!"

And it was as though Secret understood what Angus had asked. He surged forward, his power far beyond his relatively small stature, and Alice only had to touch him with her heels to put him into a canter. Keeping her hands featherlight, sitting up straight, Alice couldn't help but grin as Secret bounded towards the coloured fences, taking off perfectly, knowing Alice wouldn't hold him back as he soared over the green and white poles, at one with his rider as they seemed to turn in the air and on to the next jump. Alice thought that there really was no better feeling, as each fence disappeared under Secret's neat pale hooves. She might be jumping against the likes of Leah Edwards and their sponsored ponies, but she knew there was no pony she'd rather have than Secret. Every tear shed, every moment she'd felt like giving up, it had all been worth it, for this.

Time passed quickly by; short, cold days that meant Alice didn't really see Secret in daylight. Fitness with Secret had been stepped up, and Josephine had been leading him around the lanes and up the steep hill overlooking the downs while she rode Ella and Alice went to school. And now there were merely days left until end of term, when they'd leave for London.

Alice's classmates chatted incessantly about Christmas shopping and who was going to the most Christmas parties. But as the bell rang for the final time that year, Alice had practically sprinted down the steps and on to the bus, giving her classmates a quick wave goodbye as they continued their plans for the holidays. For Alice, it was all about Olympia and Secret now.

★

Alice's mobile rang the next morning as she was mucking out. Peeling gloves off frozen fingers to answer, she frowned as she missed the call. Almost immediately a text followed.

Alice, it's Celia, the message read, and Alice frowned again. *Give me a call when you have a chance X*

Alice's brain went into overdrive as she tried to imagine why Celia, leader of the Rebel Riders, wanted her to call. An icy hand gripped her spine:

what if Finn had fallen, had some sort of terrible accident? Sitting down on a hay bale, she dialled the number Celia had left with a shaking hand.

"Alice!" Celia's voice, with its strong Spanish accent that evoked a rich image of the warmth of her home country, answered straight away. "How are you?"

"I'm fine," Alice stammered. "Is everything OK? Is it about Finn? Has something happened?"

"No." Celia chuckled. "He's fine! I wanted to let you know that I have a spare backstage pass for the next few days," she explained. "Full access, everything. You can watch the shows right from the warm-up with all the top riders. Fancy it?"

There was nothing Alice would have liked more. She'd never really got to experience Olympia fully, having always had a pony of her mum's or her mum's clients to ride, and they were there and back in a day. She'd watched the Grand Prix dressage and the puissance on TV, and had always longed to see it in real life. But she couldn't take Celia up on her offer.

"That sounds amazing," she said longingly. "But I can't. I have to carry on my work with Secret, and Mum needs me here." Although Fergus was coming back from his trip home the following evening, there were still so many chores to be done.

"I understand," Celia said. "But if you wanted, you could have one of our stables in this yard we're currently at when we move our horses to Olympia. I checked with the stable manager – you could bring Secret here and have a couple of days enjoying the show before you moved him to his Olympia stable." She paused. "There's some other riders here doing the same. I think they are about your age. No idea who they are but I think they might be showjumpers. It's in Hyde Park, amazing hacking."

Alice imagined her and Secret in London. It sounded pretty tempting – maybe it wouldn't hurt just to *mention* it to her mum? Even if she somehow managed just one day, it would still be amazing.

"Well, think about it," Celia said, sensing her thoughts. "We'd all love to see you. Especially Finn!" And Alice blushed happily.

Chapter 4

"Well, I actually think it's a wonderful idea."

Josephine caught Alice totally by surprise later as they cleared up after dinner. Alice had just mentioned her conversation with Celia, not expecting her mum to say she could go!

"Secret is happy wherever he goes," Alice's mum continued. "And I think you really deserve it. You've been a huge help these past few weeks while Fergus has been away, and I know it hasn't been easy juggling your school work with your jump training." She smiled at Alice as she filled the kettle. "Let me make a couple of phone calls. You remember my godmother Emily, my old instructor? She lives just round the corner from those stables. In fact, I'm sure she used to teach there. She's always said we would be welcome to go and stay."

And as her mum chattered away to Emily on the phone, leaving Alice in no doubt that her mum's godmother had agreed, the week she'd been looking forward to ever since that hot August day moved even closer!

True to her word, Alice's mum had it sorted by the following morning. Alice could stay with Emily, who lived a five-minute walk from the stables at Hyde Park. And the stable manager, who it turned out knew Josephine from years ago, was happy for Secret to occupy one of the stables vacated by the Rebel Riders. Olympia was due to start the next day and the Rebel Riders were in the process of moving their team ponies and Horatio over to the Olympia stables for the week so that they could perform their daily show. Alice had looked up the yard in Hyde Park on the Internet, admiring the enormous stables and sand track around the famous park.

"And you'll never guess what," Alice's mum had smiled as she finished the final phone call. "That young showjumper who was in *Pony* mag recently, the sponsored one, is at the same yard! Leah Edwards?"

"Yes, that's right!" Alice said, feeling a jolt of excitement. She imagined her and Leah hacking together through the park … making friends. She couldn't wait! "Thanks so much, Mum," she added. "I really appreciate it."

"It's fine." Alice's mum gave her a hug. "As I said yesterday, you've worked so hard. And these sorts of opportunities don't come along very often!" Then she grinned. "We'd better get packing!"

Josephine's lorry pulled away from Park Farm the very next afternoon, at the same time as Finn and the Rebel Riders were making their debut in the big arena prior to the evening Grand Prix dressage. Alice had texted Finn to wish him luck but not heard anything back, figuring he was probably busy with the preparations.

Alice had hurriedly packed a suitcase and Secret's trunk and all the bits she needed for the big class. Secret had practically skipped up the ramp, nudging Alice as she tied him up and giving her the expression that never failed to bring a lump to her throat, his big brown eyes soft and trusting as he seemed to ask her *where are we heading this time?*

"On another big adventure, boy!" She hugged him in reply.

★

It wasn't long before the brown landscape of ploughed fields and bare hedges gave way to towns and main roads, and then the motorway stretched ahead, leading them to London. Alice and her mum chatted away in the cab, discussing Alice's feelings about the upcoming class, working out strategies for keeping Secret as calm and focused as possible.

It seemed no time at all before the big horse lorry was crawling through stop–start traffic as they reached central London, standing out against an endless sea of black cabs, double-decker buses, and the blur of police and ambulance lights. Craning her neck, Alice stared out of the window as her mum pointed out Hyde Park. The enormous expanse of land stretched out, punctuated by huge trees and ringed by a wide path where joggers wearing earphones ran alongside dog walkers and children on bikes. And there were some horses! Walking calmly along the sand track that lay parallel to the path were a big grey and an enormous dark bay, their riders in the fluorescent uniform of the mounted police. Alice admired the way they walked quietly past a yapping dog and several joggers. She wondered how Secret was going to react to it all!

"Oh, look, Emily's come to meet us!" Alice's mum smiled as she indicated down a side street and eased the lorry through some big gates into the smartest-looking yard Alice had seen. A wiry lady in her sixties, wearing breeches and a smart duffel jacket, gave them a wave. Alice hadn't seen her mum's godmother for a few years, but she hadn't changed and always looked as though

she was just about to hack out with the queen. She was kind too, even lending Finn and Sasha a side saddle when theirs had been destroyed in the fire at Rookham Manor.

"Hi, Emily." Josephine hugged her godmother. "Thanks so much for this."

Alice gave Emily a hug, feeling a little shy and suddenly aware her mum was going to leave her soon and she'd be on her own, but Emily's smile was warm and welcoming.

"Oh, it's lovely to have you here!" Emily laughed. "But I'm afraid I'm not going to be much of a host as I've a busy few days. I'll leave you with a key and a well-stocked fridge, but your mum tells me you'll either be here at the yard or at Olympia, is that right?"

"Yes, thank you," Alice said, feeling relieved. As nice as Emily was, she didn't want to be sitting in her house for hours making polite conversation.

Horsey and no-nonsense, Emily seemed the type who would largely leave her to it, and that suited Alice just fine!

Alice felt extra proud as she led Secret down the ramp. He looked amazing. His green rug perfectly set off the red of his coat, and his silken mane lifted in the cold breeze as he surveyed his new surroundings. Bright eyed, he followed Alice eagerly into the yard.

The yard manager, a woman about Alice's mum's age, strode forward, warmly greeting them and quickly reminiscing with Josephine about their old showjumping days. Then she turned to Alice with a smile.

"I'm Clare," she said in a friendly voice. "It's fantastic you're following in your mum's showjumping footsteps!"

Alice glanced briefly at her mum, who had a wistful look on her face, and just for a second

Alice wondered if it brought back some painful memories. Josephine had stopped riding altogether after her star pony, Blue, was injured and had to retire early.

"It's wonderful," Josephine said. "And I think Alice and Secret are going to go much, much further than I did too!"

Clare showed Alice to her stable, a brick-built corner stable with the original cobbled floor. It was just like the yard at Rookham Manor, and Alice imagined all the decades of horses that had come and gone before Secret. His hooves made a satisfying *clip-clop* on the cobbles and an immaculate shavings bed had been made up in preparation. Secret immediately rolled, coating his rug with shavings, before tucking into the sweetest-smelling hay net.

Alice smiled and then looked up as a girl approached the stable next to hers, leading the most gorgeous skewbald pony whose dark-brown patches shone like conkers. The pony had his head held high, trembling as he gazed all around him, spooking slightly at unknown objects as he let out a startled whinny. The girl leading him placed a hand on his neck as if to reassure him, and the pony relaxed slightly.

A scarlet saddlecloth emblazoned *Hadley Feeds* left Alice in no doubt that this had to be Leah Edwards and her sponsored pony, Red Kite B, affectionately known as Kite, according to the article in *Pony* magazine. Alice waved in greeting. Leah had looked so friendly in the magazine photos. But the girl just removed her hat and shook out her mane of auburn hair, which almost perfectly matched the conker brown of Kite's skewbald patches, and gave the briefest nod in response.

"Leah, this is Alice, from the Hilltops branch,"

Clare said. "Alice, Leah is from the Clere Forest branch. She's been down here for a couple of weeks with an instructor."

Wow, Alice thought. Leah must be amazing. To have sponsorship and a private instructor was some investment, and despite looking quite highly strung, Kite was even more gorgeous in real life.

"I've not heard of your branch," she said in a friendly voice.

Leah fixed her with a cold stare. "Well, no," she replied. "You probably haven't because it's a pony club centre, part of a riding school. Not like Hilltops."

Alice realised her mistake. Leah must think she was part of some really snobby, cliquey pony crowd.

"Oh no, it's not that," she said hurriedly. "I'm totally new to pony club. I actually just joined at the start of the year. I don't know any of the branches, really. I'm still working it all out."

"Oh," Leah said, looking at Secret, who was hanging his head over the stable door with interest, snow-white shavings tangled in his red forelock. "You've climbed up the ranks quickly then." And with that Leah turned back to her pony.

Unsure if this was a compliment or not, and feeling slightly intimidated, Alice just gave a small smile and nodded. Perhaps they weren't going to be friends after all.

Chapter 5

Once Secret was settled, Josephine helped Alice carry her bags to Emily's beautiful white house on the corner of Hyde Park. And then it was time to say goodbye. Alice gave her mum a huge hug, wishing she could stay with her, but knowing Josephine had to get back to the ponies at home. As her mum eased the lorry out of the gates of the yard, waving goodbye, Alice realised with a jolt that the next time she would see her, she'd be loading Secret up to take him across London to his Olympia stable!

★

By the evening, Alice was starting to get her bearings. Emily had sat down with her and gone through the journey to Olympia several times, and Alice had written down the bus and tube routes. She'd been back and forth to check on Secret. The light had already been fading by the time they'd arrived so she'd not been able to ride, but Alice had made sure she'd given the little gelding a really good groom, enjoying the shine the brushes brought to his red coat.

Emily had made her cheese on toast for dinner and then Alice had gone back to the yard for a final evening visit before the big gates were locked. The area Emily lived in was very pretty, but it was slightly disconcerting navigating the short walk down the pavement towards the yard. It seemed as though the traffic never stopped, the orange glow of headlights almost blinding Alice as she pulled her scarf up around her nose. The yard was a little sanctuary among the hustle and bustle of the city. The park was still busy, street lights illuminating the wide path as joggers continued to run up and down, and couples strolled by arm in arm with tiny dogs on leads.

Leah was in the yard when Alice arrived, smiling as Secret whickered at her. Happy anywhere, he'd obviously been having a snooze after his evening feed and scrambled to his feet in greeting. Leah was fussing over Kite, who was fidgeting next door, wrapping scarlet bandages around his slim legs for the night, which were also emblazoned with the gold embroidery of Hadley Feeds. It was almost like Kite and Leah were a brand in themselves, the dramatic auburn of Leah's hair and Kite's gleaming conker patches making them a truly stunning pairing. And everything they used was top end and labelled with the sponsor's name. No wonder they had such a following. Alice cleared her throat, aware that with the old-fashioned bars between the stables they could clearly see each other.

"You've done amazingly, getting such a good sponsorship deal," she said, and Leah looked up, as if she'd just noticed Alice was there. "Kite is so lovely."

"Thanks," Leah muttered, concentrating on her tasks.

There was a short pause.

"I'd love it if a big company approached me," Alice continued, thinking about her own dreams. "I'd *love* to be a sponsored rider."

Leah fixed her with a cool gaze. "Why?" she said. "Your mum is Josephine Smalley, right? So why do you need sponsorship?"

Alice flushed. It was true she didn't have to worry about livery costs or entry fees.

"I mean … um…" She tried to explain herself. "More that it would mean I've really made it. For someone to want me on their team, I guess."

Leah shrugged. "Well," she said. "If *I* had it my own way, it would just be me and Kite. But I can't be like you, can I? I don't get to choose my own path."

She turned her back on Alice, and carried on her chores in silence. Alice frowned, but reasoned that she was going to be competing against her very soon, so maybe Leah was professional enough not to get friendly with any of her rivals. And tomorrow Alice would be seeing Finn anyway, and enjoying the backstage pass Celia had given her. It didn't matter if she didn't make any new friends, this once.

★

Alice had a restless night's sleep. Used to the countryside of home, where the only sounds were the occasional pony snort or the hoot of an owl, she'd eventually pulled the pillow over her ears to block out the sounds of traffic. However, drawing back her curtains the next morning, she was captivated by the sight of the park glittering with frost in the first tendrils of the morning sun. She had the whole morning to spend with Secret before making her way over to Olympia on the carefully planned route Emily had worked out for her. Throwing on her jodhpurs and a warm jumper she headed down to the kitchen, where there was a note waiting for her.

Morning Alice, Emily's neat handwriting read. *I've gone to my exercise class, then I'm out most of the day. I'm going to watch the dressage at Olympia later so can meet you there to come home with you. Plenty of food, help yourself!*

Gosh, Alice thought in awe. Emily really was an early bird! After two slices of toast she headed down to the yard, where Clare greeted her with a smile.

"Just done my morning checks," she said warmly. "Your pony's a character, isn't he?"

Alice chuckled. "You could say that!"

"Now is the best time to ride, if you want to head out," Clare continued. "There will be some joggers out but it's too cold and early yet for most. I'll get you a map of the park."

"Thank you!" Alice smiled. She'd been longing to hack Secret around the famous park. It was a beautiful winter's morning, the pink sun now having crept on to the horizon, the city stretching and awakening with it.

Kite was gone from his stable, his head collar looped on the ring next to his door. Secret whinnied, as if displeased his new next-door neighbour had disappeared.

"Is Leah riding out as well?" Alice asked, wondering if she might catch her up. Although Leah was not exactly friendly, it would be nice for both ponies to have company in the new hacking environment, and Kite seemed on edge, so it might do him good to have another pony with him.

"No, not exactly," Clare explained. "She's having some sort of promotional photo shoot in the park. I had to let them all in extra early."

"Oh, right." Alice thought back to her conversation with Leah the previous evening. She'd been so spiky when she'd mentioned her sponsorship. But to Alice, photo shoots and top-of-the-range rugs and bandages seemed like a very good deal!

Swinging herself lightly into her saddle a short while later, Alice tucked the map Clare had given her into her pocket. It was fairly simple: she had to stick to the wide sand path and be courteous to other park users. There were some parts of the path that were busier than others, sections that went past the lake and main roads, and quieter, almost forest-like areas. A mist hung over the lake and the park was quiet, just as Clare said it would be, apart from the odd runner or dog walker clutching a steaming takeaway cup of coffee.

Secret set off at a jog before settling into a relaxed walk. Alice remembered Angus's words, about allowing Secret some downtime before the pressures of the weekend, and made sure she let Secret have a loose rein. The sand was beautifully maintained and Secret's pale hooves barely made a sound as they rode on, enjoying the sights and sounds of the park.

Then Alice blinked. Up ahead there was some

sort of hold-up on the wide path next to the lake. A whole team of people and equipment, including the light reflectors Alice recognised from her time in France, when Secret had trotted straight through a fashion magazine shoot. She realised she knew the pony standing in the middle of it all, a gorgeous skewbald, his auburn-haired rider in polished boots and the scarlet jacket emblazoned with her sponsor's name. It was Leah and Kite.

But before Alice could get any closer, a shortish, plump man with black slicked hair and an air of superiority put a hand up.

"Wait there just a minute, young lady," he said in a bored tone, without even looking at Alice. "Wait until we've got our last photo, would you? Don't want you upsetting our Kite."

Too taken aback to do anything else, Alice did as she was told and halted Secret while the photographer clicked away. Alice looked at Leah, who seemed tense. Kite was flinging his head around, dancing on the spot, clearly unhappy with the proceedings.

"Leah, crack a smile," the man snapped, and Leah did as she was told, but it was probably the most insincere smile Alice had ever seen. "You're meant to be the pony club superstar," the man continued. "*Act* like it. And keep that pony still for one second, would you?" His tone had an edge to it and Alice frowned, wondering who on earth he was and why he was able to talk to Leah that way.

Like Kite, Leah obviously wasn't happy. Holding her hand up, she glared at the man as the photographer lowered the camera with an irritated look on his face.

"What?" the man snapped.

"Kite's not himself," Leah said firmly. "He's not

been happy since we got here. I think this is all too much. I should be just hacking him, keeping him relaxed at this stage. Not posing for photos."

Alice wasn't sure if she'd imagined it but she thought Leah threw a longing glance in her direction as she said this. Unsure what to do, she patted Secret. She was desperate to continue her hack around the park, and didn't want to turn back, but the group were blocking her way. She sat and waited.

"And *I* own him," the man said darkly. "So you'll do as I say."

So this was Kite and Leah's sponsor, Alice realised. He seemed horrible! Despite how frosty Leah had been the day before, Alice felt a little sorry for her. They were obviously all having a bad day. Finally she was free to pass the crowd and she and Secret set off again, but not before Alice glanced back and just for a second caught

Leah's eye. The other girl wore an expression Alice couldn't quite work out. It was like she was trapped. But, just as quickly, Leah looked away and the moment was gone.

Chapter 6

After mucking out and allowing Secret a brief turn-out in the small paddock adjacent to the yard, it was time for Alice to rush back and change, ready to catch the bus to Olympia to watch Finn's display.

The bus was easier to manage than Alice had thought. The stop was just a few metres from Emily's front door, and the Travelcard her mum had organised for her worked, much to Alice's relief. She climbed upstairs, enjoying the view of the city as the bus wound its way through the streets. Everywhere was so Christmassy. The big familiar signs outside Olympia sent a little shiver down Alice's spine and she couldn't stop the butterflies in her stomach as she passed the trade stands and headed towards the stables and the welcome aroma of hay and shavings and horses.

She quickly found Finn. He was sitting on a tack trunk, dressed and ready in his Rebel Riders' costume. The Flying Fillies always looked amazing, but the Rebel Riders, with their very own dressmaker on the team, took it to another level. Finn was in a dark-blue military-style jacket with gold piping and a stiff collar, his long legs encased in breeches and leather boots brought over from Spain. As she approached Alice thought how handsome he looked. He continued to laugh and chat with the other riders, unaware she was there. But as she got nearer he gave a start, jumping to his feet and hugging her. Although it had only been two weeks since she'd seen him last, and she'd been so busy with her Olympia prep, Alice realised just how much she really had missed him.

"Hey!" Finn released her with a grin. "You made it! So good to see you."

"And you." Alice grinned, aware of the smiles from the other Rebel Riders.

Finn took Alice's hand and led the way to Horatio's stable so she could see how the gorgeous snow-white Highland was getting on. Incredibly calm by nature, he was munching on a hay net, as if being stabled at the world's biggest horse show was no big deal.

"How did Secret settle in at Hyde Park?" Finn asked as they leaned on the door. "The yard's amazing, isn't it?"

"Yes! And you know Secret," Alice chuckled. "Happy wherever he goes. We had a lovely early morning ride around the park today. London's actually really pretty from horseback!"

"It's cool, isn't it?" Finn agreed. "Hey, did you meet that other showjumper yet? I never really got a chance to say hello. Leah somebody or other, has a lovely pony, but he was too spooked to come near any of us."

"Yeah." Alice frowned, thinking back to her slightly weird encounter with Leah that morning and the rude man in the park. "But she's not very friendly."

Finn shrugged. "You *are* rivals, I guess."

Leah was forgotten then as Celia swept over and hugged Alice before chivvying Finn along to get Horatio out of the stable and into the warm-up ring. Alice watched the Rebel Riders canter around the small ring in their normal relaxed manner before she made her way down the famous tunnel towards the entrance to the huge international arena, finding a quiet spot to stand and watch. Even today, not actually competing, it gave her goose bumps as the arena opened up in front of her.

"Ladies and gentlemen, boys and girls!" The loudspeaker boomed as the famous Olympia music started to play. "They went down a storm yesterday on their debut and we are so pleased to have them here this week, all the way from Spain … the Rebel Riders!"

Alice clapped along with the crowd, and as the team galloped in she had never felt so proud. The Wednesday crowd was mainly made up of dressage enthusiasts, but they were soon cheering loudly as the riders performed all manner of daring tricks, including Finn's trademark gallop across the arena hanging upside down. The applause was almost deafening as Celia finished with a spectacular capriole on her gorgeous grey horse, Domino.

"Wow!" Alice ran alongside Finn as he trotted back in, dark hair damp with sweat, a grin on his face. "That was incredible!"

She was still buzzing a while later as she helped Finn sponge Horatio down before rugging him up and leading him round to gently warm down. When Finn was called over by Celia for a chat, Alice happily agreed to put Horatio back in his stable. She knew the sweet gelding well, from all her visits to Rookham Manor.

Just as she'd shut the stable door after giving Horatio a pat and making sure he had enough hay, she spotted something on the floor. Some sort of bracelet with a pony-head charm attached, glinting in the sand. Picking it up, Alice approached the stable next door, clearing her throat nervously.

What if it was Charlotte Dujardin or John Whitaker in there? Whoever was in the stable had obviously not long arrived, judging by the tack trunks piled up outside the door. The sweet bay mare who popped her head over to say hello seemed awfully familiar, Alice suddenly thought, stopping in her tracks. It couldn't be, could it? Then the smiling face appeared, long golden hair in a sleek ponytail. It was Devon Jenkins, her hero!

"Hey!"

"Hi ... um..." Alice felt as if her mouth was full of concrete, unable to make any words. Instead she thrust the bracelet forward. "Found this... Is it yours?"

Devon's pretty face lit up. "Oh my gosh!" she cried in a relieved tone. "Yes, it is! That's my bracelet!"

Alice handed it over, pleased she could help.

"Thanks so much," Devon continued. "Honestly,

I wouldn't have been able to jump without it." She pointed to the little charm on the delicate silver chain. "It brings me luck, and I'm *so* superstitious!"

Devon was so friendly, Alice immediately felt at ease.

"It's no problem," she smiled. "Glad you got it back."

"I must have dropped it when I was unloading stuff," Devon said. Then she looked at Horatio, who'd put his handsome head over the door to investigate. "Sweet pony!" she cried. "Is he yours? Do you work for that amazing display team? I just saw the last bit. I could hear all this cheering so I went down to see what was going on."

"No, not exactly," Alice replied, swelling with pride as she thought of Devon watching Finn ride. "I'm just here to watch. He belongs to my … friend."

She thought about saying boyfriend, but she

was never really sure what she and Finn were. Closer than friends, perhaps, but they'd never really put a label on their relationship.

"Oh, cool," Devon smiled. "So I'll see you about? What's your name? I'm Devon."

"I know." Alice blushed. "My name's Alice." Then before she could stop herself, she told Devon she was jumping on Sunday. She longed to talk showjumping with someone as cool as Devon. "My pony, he's coming here on Saturday," she said, all in a rush. "We qualified in the summer for the Pony Club Christmas Tree Stakes, it's been amazing."

For a minute Devon's eyes seemed to cloud over, and Alice wondered if she'd somehow said the wrong thing, but what? However, Devon's expression quickly changed to a megawatt smile.

"Lovely," she said kindly. "That's the class I did

on my first trip to Olympia." She lifted up the bracelet to the light and gently touched the little pony charm. "I rode an amazing pony called The Talisman. But..." She looked as though she was going to say something else, then shook her head. "Anyway, this is my own little talisman, to bring me luck."

Chapter 7

"What a wonderful evening!"

Alice was glad of Emily's company on the journey back to Hyde Park. It was one thing catching the bus on her own on a bright winter's afternoon, but quite another in the dark. Emily was very smartly dressed, having enjoyed the Kur, the dressage to music, from a private box. Alice and Finn had shared pizza together backstage, watching from the warm-up ring. It had been magical and awe-inspiring to see the world's greatest dressage riders perform their tests to thundering music, and Alice still had stars in her eyes when she found Emily at the end. From her hack in the park, and then watching Finn ride, to meeting Devon and watching the dressage, it had been one of the best days she'd had in ages!

"Just enough time to pop in and see Secret on the way back." Emily checked her watch. "I'll come with you."

It was new having Secret at a livery yard, but Clare didn't offer any sort of DIY arrangement. Alice was grateful; it meant she'd been able to enjoy Olympia without worrying about who was going to feed or skip out Secret, but equally it was strange when she was used to doing everything herself!

"What was it like backstage?" Emily asked.

"Really interesting," Alice replied. "Seeing all the preparations going on."

"Ooh," Emily said, her eyes twinkling. "Meet anyone famous?"

"Actually, yes!" Alice enthused, and told Emily how Devon Jenkins was stabling her horse next to Finn's pony.

Emily frowned, as if trying to remember something.

"Devon Jenkins. Yes, she's doing very well, isn't she," she said. "She came from nowhere, you know. Talent-spotted at a riding school. Then there was that dreadful business with her pony. She's done fantastically well to get herself back up the levels again. Always did admire a gutsy rider."

Alice thought about the little talisman on Devon's bracelet. A talisman for a talisman, she'd said. Again, Alice wondered why she'd looked so sad when she'd mentioned the pony's name.

Secret was lying down in his enormous stable and didn't get up as Alice turned his light on, giving a low rumbly whicker in welcome instead. Alice added another wafer of hay to his net and topped up his water bucket as Emily looked on, out of place in her evening dress. From the next stable along Kite reached over the door and Emily leaned over to pat his handsome head.

Then she looked closer, and frowned. "I recognise that rug," she said, her brow furrowed. "Hadley. I'm sure this is the same company that used to sponsor Devon." She paused. "That's why I admired her so. Although she was dropped so suddenly, she managed to start over. It just seemed so unfair, but I guess they didn't get on. That's what I heard, anyway."

"What happened to her pony?" Alice asked curiously, thinking back to the way Devon's eyes had clouded over when she'd handed her the bracelet.

"Well, he was injured, in a horsebox, as I recall," Emily replied. "I remember the report in *Horse & Hound*. He had to be put down." She shook her head. "Poor Devon. He was quite a pony, The Talisman, just on the verge of the big time. I'm glad she managed to make it anyway. Awful for her, losing her pony, then getting dropped by her sponsors like that."

No wonder Devon had looked so upset when she thought about her old pony, Alice thought. She knew just how hard it was to lose a pony you loved. Then she thought back to her odd encounter with Leah in the park, and the obvious tension between her and Kite's owner, who must have been the same man who'd owned Devon's pony, The Talisman.

But as Secret stretched out luxuriously, Alice

shrugged. She was jumping *against* Leah on Sunday, so perhaps best to stay away.

★

The next day Alice was planning to spend the day with Secret and then return to Olympia for the evening performance. Waking early, the city buzzing behind her window, Alice called her mum, as she'd promised to each morning.

"Alice!" Her mum sounded pleased. "How was yesterday?"

Alice told her all about the ride, and the wonderful afternoon at Olympia.

As she rang off, her phone pinged with a new message. Finn.

Got some time free this morning, the text read. *Fancy an adventure?*

Intrigued, Alice messaged back.

What sort of adventure?

Her phone pinged again almost immediately.

Meet me at the Natural History Museum at 10, Finn's reply read. *And wear something warm.*

Alice checked her map, deciding she'd go there straight after seeing Secret. Opening her suitcase, she pulled out a pair of jeans and her thickest, warmest jumper before quickly dressing and heading down to the yard. It was even colder than the day before and a heavy mist hung low over the park, a hard frost making everything glitter and sparkle.

Leah arrived at the stables as the same time as Alice, stamping her feet and blowing on to her hands as they waited for Clare to unlock the gates.

"Hey," Alice said in a friendly voice, and Leah gave a half-smile in response.

"Morning."

Thinking the other girl seemed slightly nicer today, Alice continued to chat as they made their way over to their stables.

"How is Kite settling in?" she asked as they each set to work on mucking out.

Leah frowned. "He's nervy by nature," she said. "But he's been on edge since getting here, worse than normal."

"Oh," Alice said, looking at Secret, who was dreamily tucking into his breakfast, eyes closed. "Maybe it's the big occasion coming up." She gulped. It was a big occasion for *her* as well. She quickly changed the subject as she felt her tummy start to flutter.

"Maybe," Leah said, but she sounded unconvinced.

"Are you riding today?" Alice asked, and Leah nodded.

"I've got a lesson with my trainer this morning," she said. "And then I've got to go over to Olympia. Nick – he's the one who sorts my sponsorship – wants me on the stand for a bit."

"Ooh," Alice said, her eyes widening. "That's cool! I saw Charlotte Dujardin on her sponsor's stand yesterday. The queue was miles long! Is it really exciting? You must feel like a star!"

Leah paused, and her face clouded over for a second. "I guess," she said quietly.

Fluffing up the banks of the shavings bed as Secret licked out his feed bucket, Alice paused, leaning on her fork. She hoped Leah would see that she wasn't in any way snobby, just really interested in her riding career.

"I met Devon Jenkins yesterday," she said. "Her horse is stabled next to my friend's pony. She was so nice!"

Leah's eyes widened as she looked around her, almost as if to check no one was listening in.

"I'm not allowed to talk about Devon," she said in a low voice. "Nick says she went off the rails after her pony was put down, refused to go to any events or try out any more ponies so they had to get rid of her. He said she twisted the story and made *them* look like the bad guys. Please don't mention her to me again."

★

Alice couldn't stop thinking about Devon and The Talisman as she made her way to meet Finn. However, she was soon distracted as she hopped off the bus outside the Natural History Museum.

Looking up, she stood in awe for a minute as she gazed at the huge building, and the Christmas tree in the centre of the ice rink. It suddenly dawned on her that Finn was taking her ice skating, and she inwardly groaned. She'd never been before, and despite her natural balance on her horse, her long legs meant she could be a little uncoordinated in other sports. She was a terrible runner and hockey player at school, tripping over her own feet far too many times. And Finn would probably be amazing. She rolled her eyes at the thought. Finn appeared with a big grin on his face, clutching two tickets.

"Ready?" He chuckled at the expression on Alice's face.

"Not funny," Alice huffed. "I've never been skating before. I'm going to be terrible!"

Finn shook his head. "You'll be fine!" he said. "I've never been before either. Some of the guys from the Rebel Riders came the other night and said how fun it was so I thought we should give it a go. Come on!"

And so a short time later, the ice-skating boots heavy and unwieldy on her feet, Alice wobbled her way out on to the rink, clutching the side unsteadily. A girl whizzed past and, gritting her teeth, Alice carefully pushed herself away from the side and tried to copy her. For one awful moment she felt herself topple, but steadied herself, pushing her feet forward, until suddenly she was gliding.

"Hey!" she called triumphantly behind her to Finn. "I can do it!"

But turning, she had to suppress her giggles as she saw Finn clutching on to the side, his feet slipping wildly all over the place. Turning a wide, smooth circle, Alice skated easily back to him.

"Want a hand?" she grinned.

The hour wasn't long enough. Alice got better and better, gliding around, attempting some spins, the power and the exhilaration almost as good as riding Secret. Finn had eventually wobbled around the Christmas tree before Alice took his hand and together they circled the rink.

"Think I'll stick with horses!" At least Finn was laughing about being so rubbish, Alice thought, as they clutched a hot chocolate in the café later.

"Probably for the best." She grinned, and he

prodded her arm playfully in response. It was really nice, Alice thought, just hanging out with him. They'd shared a kiss in France, but since then had just enjoyed each other's company, without any awkwardness or unanswered questions.

Finn smiled and checked his watch. "I don't have to be back at Olympia until half two," he said. "Let's go back to the stables. I want to see how Secret is getting on in the big city!"

Chapter 8

Alice was still rosy-cheeked and buzzing from ice skating as she skipped through the yard gates a little later.

"Finn!" Clare greeted them with a big smile. "How is it going at Olympia?"

"Brilliant, thanks," Finn replied. "Just having a break and seeing how Secret's getting on."

"Oh, we'll miss him when he goes!" Clare

laughed. "He's wonderful. Alice, are you riding now?" Alice nodded as Clare continued. "Finn, do you want to join her? You can ride Mr Perkins."

"Sure," Finn said. "Thanks, Clare."

"Honestly." Alice raised an eyebrow as Clare moved on to her next task. "Is there anyone you meet who doesn't allow you to ride their horses?"

Finn laughed. "No," he said. "But aren't you glad? It'll be cool to ride together round Hyde Park."

And Alice had to agree, it was. It was more than cool, in fact. It was downright amazing!

★

Mr Perkins was a gorgeous bay ex-show horse with the softest brown eyes. Soon Alice and Finn were riding out side by side, Secret's jaunty walk matching the long, relaxed strides of Mr Perkins. The park was busier than the day before as it was later in the morning, but Secret was taking it all in his stride. They rode in contented silence, or chatting away, both at their most comfortable together in the saddle.

The route they followed took them through some huge and ancient beech tree woods. Frost still clung to the shady patches and the ponies' breath hung in the air. It had been a little while since the hot chocolate at the skating rink, and as they passed a pretty wooden cabin, Alice thought it was definitely time for another hot drink.

Jumping down, Alice passed her reins over to Finn and paid for a hot chocolate, enjoying the moment as she took back Secret's reins and sipped her drink, relishing their little oasis in the bustling city. It was perfect until Secret gave her a sharp nudge and she tipped the drink over her arm.

"Oh, Secret!" Clumsily, Alice tried to save the rest of her hot chocolate as Finn chuckled. But suddenly Secret was free, Alice's hands having let go of the reins for a second. She made a grab for him but it was too late. Secret had already seen something in the distance that looked far more exciting…

Nudging Mr Perkins with urgency, Finn set off after Secret at a brisk trot as Alice ran behind, still clutching her cup, her heart beating in her chest and sweat prickling down her back, despite the icy chill. It was one thing Secret getting loose at a show, like he had done all that time ago, but this was far more serious. They were right in the middle of London, with traffic surrounding the park on all sides.

Alice's panic grew as she kept running, the sleek brown back of Mr Perkins in front of her getting smaller as Finn tried to catch up with Secret. Joggers paused as they surveyed the strange scene, a red pony cantering loose followed by a big horse … followed by a red-faced Alice. Luckily

Secret was sticking to the horse track, so no one was having to dive out of his way, but if Secret darted out he could easily escape into the streets, where he could cause a serious accident, or even be killed.

Then Alice became aware of an unexpected sound: laughter. A large group of tourists were pointing and smiling, cameras clicking as they jostled for a better view. Finn had stopped Mr Perkins up ahead and seemed completely speechless. In front of them were six huge horses, dwarfing even Mr Perkins, riding two by two and in complete sync. Their double bridles gleamed, and their riders wore smart black breeches and bright-yellow jackets. The only thing out of place was a small red pony trotting proudly between them, reins clutched by the rider on the lead horse. It was Secret, and he was with the mounted police!

For a few seconds, time stood still. The laughter from the tourists had grown louder, and now quite a crowd had gathered as the police riders neared Alice, who stood frozen to the spot. If ponies could smile, then Secret would have the biggest grin on his face, she thought. He looked so proud, barely reaching the police horses' saddles, but still matching them stride for stride.

"Is this your pony?" A kindly-looking older man with twinkling blue eyes stopped in front of Alice, as Secret stopped smartly as well, almost as if in salute. Reaching up, the little red gelding gave the big bay next to him an affectionate nibble on his neck as the horse, ever the professional, tried to ignore him.

"Y … yes…" Alice could barely stammer. What if they arrested her? Was that possible? Public disorder or something. Did they arrest ponies?

"Well now," the policeman smiled. "He knows

his own mind, this one. He came straight for us!"

"I'm so sorry," Alice mumbled. "Thanks so much for bringing him back."

"It's all right." The policewoman on the other side, a younger lady with blonde hair tied neatly in a bun, smiled. "We do all sorts in our job. Catching little roan ponies is not the everyday, though!"

"Where are you heading?" the policeman asked.

"Back to the Hyde Park stables," Alice said, feeling a wave of relief that they weren't cross or, indeed, about to arrest her. Finn rode up on Mr Perkins as Alice patted Secret before swinging back up into the saddle.

"Ah, yes, Clare's place." The policeman nodded. "We're heading that way. We'll escort you there! I'm Officer Hill, and this is my colleague Officer Fairbanks. But you can call us Edward and Rosie."

And so they headed off, quite the sight – six beautiful police horses, a large show horse and little Secret, who jogged next to the lead police horses, clearly delighted with himself at having caused this adventure.

"What brings you to Hyde Park?" Rosie asked. "I've not seen your pony before. We get to know who's who at Clare's."

"Olympia," Alice said with a note of pride. "Both me and Finn are riding there." She gestured at Finn. "Finn is in a display team and I'm showjumping on Sunday."

Sunday... Alice realised with a jolt. So close now. Her time in London was flying by.

"Marvellous." Edward smiled. "Your pony might be cheeky but he must be talented! You'll see our colleagues doing their display at Olympia. We're all going to watch them at the weekend so I'll look out for your class, and your display." He nodded at Finn.

First the whole pony club branch, Alice thought,

now the mounted police! The pressure was truly on…

"OK," she croaked. "I'm jumping in the Pony Club Christmas Tree Stakes."

They soon reached Clare's yard, and just as Alice and Finn were about to peel off, a familiar skewbald pony clattered by, clad in a scarlet exercise rug. Despite just having had a lesson, the handsome pony looked as highly strung as ever. Alice wasn't sure if she was imagining things but as Leah rode past she swore she saw a look pass between Rosie and Edward.

"Hadley, Ed—" she heard Rosie say, but couldn't catch the rest of it. And then Leah and Kite were out of sight and the mounted police were waving goodbye, promising to watch Alice on Sunday.

★

Once Alice had made sure Secret was settled back in his stable she fastened his special clip to the bolt. She couldn't risk him getting loose twice in one day!

It wasn't long before Alice was back on the bus to Olympia after a quick change of clothes at Emily's house. She thought excitedly about the evening ahead. There was Finn's display to watch, of course, but also the first of the big showjumping classes. Reaching the show, Alice decided that as the Rebel Riders were not on for a bit, she'd head into the shopping area and grab something to eat.

As she passed by the trade stands, her eyes were drawn to a familiar red and gold logo. Hadley Feeds. Leah was standing there looking fed up. There was a man next to her chatting animatedly with someone, the man Alice recognised from Leah's photo shoot in the park. It was Nick, the sponsor Leah had told her about. He was far more charming today than he had been then.

★ ★ ★

"Yes, we're a big believer in opportunities for young riders, especially those who wouldn't have got the chance otherwise," Nick was saying, his oily tones smooth and pleasant-sounding. "Like Leah here. She'd *never* be able to afford a pony. And now she has Red Kite B."

But something about him made Alice's skin crawl. He just seemed so insincere, and she hadn't forgotten the way he'd snapped at Leah to smile, or his threatening tone.

The man he was speaking to was obviously some sort of journalist, in his early twenties at most.

"Ah, yes. One of your most famous prodigies is doing very well now, isn't she?" he said, consulting his notepad. "Devon Jenkins is jumping here all this week. Do you regret the way things ended with her?"

"Of course, I regret how Devon took it all so badly," Nick said, his voice sounding slightly snappier. "But I'm a businessman; ponies *are* sold now and again."

The journalist frowned. "I thought The Talisman died?" He looked down at his notes again. "An accident in the lorry?"

Nick barely missed a beat but Alice noticed a look of panic cross his face before the smile reappeared. It had happened so fast, she wondered if she'd imagined it.

"Yes, of course," he said smoothly. "Devon's *main* pony, The Talisman, was put down. It was tragic, of course. She had the ride on a couple of other ponies and I was buying and selling, just like any other owner at the time. We were all *devastated* by The Talisman's death. But Devon refused to ride for us any more. I tried to explain that sometimes these things happen in the horse world, but she was young, she didn't really understand. Now," he seemed to shrug off any further mention of Devon, "can we get back to talking about our stars of *today*? Now it's all about Leah and Red Kite B…"

Chapter 9

"Hey, Alice!"

A familiar, sweet voice welcomed Alice as she waited for Finn after another brilliant Rebel Riders show. Devon Jenkins was walking her mare around, a dark-blue rug keeping the fine bay horse warm. Devon was wearing a cobalt-blue show jacket, and Alice noticed the sparkle of her little talisman on her wrist.

"If I do well tonight it's thanks to you!" Devon grinned, holding up her arm so the charm bracelet dangled down. "Are you excited about Sunday?"

"I can't wait," Alice said truthfully, although even the mere mention of the word "Sunday" was enough to make the butterflies in her tummy jangle and crash around!

Then Alice noticed Devon visibly stiffen as a figure entered the warm-up arena, kissing a nearby woman on both cheeks, laughing uproariously with a couple of men. It was Nick.

"Ugh," Devon hissed. "Why is it I can never avoid *him*?"

"He sponsors someone I know a bit," Alice said. "Leah Edwards – she rides a gorgeous pony called Kite."

Devon shook her head, disgust all over her face. "Yeah, I've seen," she snorted. "Déjà vu."

Alice frowned. Although she and Leah hadn't

got off to a great start, she remembered her trapped expression on the day of the photo shoot. And with the policewoman's comment about Hadley Feeds, and now Devon's response to the sponsor, she was starting to wonder if there was something dodgy about them.

"I'm so sorry about your pony," she blurted out, before she could stop herself. "My first pony, Honey, she died too." She closed her eyes briefly, thinking of her sweet palomino mare.

Pain flashed over Devon's face. "Thanks," she said quietly. "It still seems like yesterday. I'm sorry you lost your pony too."

"She had a heart attack," Alice said, her voice wobbling slightly. "The vet said there was nothing that could have been done."

Devon looked away. "I feel like I could have stopped Tally getting injured," she said. "If I'd been with him."

"What happened?" Alice asked.

"It was the day after getting placed at the Horse of the Year Show. Nick was annoyed I hadn't pushed Tally harder in the jump-off, but I'd done my best," Devon said flatly. "I was sixteen, too young to drive, so Nick used a transporter, a really posh one, to take him around. Anyway, I was travelling separately that day." She frowned. "I can't even remember why. I didn't usually. I think I had to sign autographs – something Nick had arranged, anyway. I didn't want to. Tally never travelled without me. He was quite nervy, but I knew how to relax him."

Alice thought about Kite, who was also highly strung but responded so well to Leah.

"He reared in the box and went over," Devon continued. "Injured himself so badly the vet had to put him down." She paused. "Nick sent me a piece of mane in the post, along with a letter to say I had been dropped from sponsorship. I was 'too difficult' to work with, he said. Because I didn't want to push Tally too hard." She snorted in disgust. "If his idea of *difficult* was questioning the welfare of my pony then so be it. I didn't care about that, but losing Tally hurt more than anything."

Alice frowned. That hadn't been the story Nick had told the journalist. She couldn't help thinking that there were more than a few similarities with Leah: a nervy pony and a rider disagreeing with the owner. And although Tally hadn't belonged to Devon, she had loved him. Like Leah and Kite.

"Maybe it's different now," Devon sighed. "But if I was your friend, I'd never let my pony out of my sight."

"What do you mean?" Alice said, but just then Nick headed their way and Devon turned her mare sharply away. Nick seemed to know everyone backstage, from the other showjumpers to the owners sipping champagne and the stewards. His voice was loud and he seemed to like the sound of it, chuckling away at his own jokes, clapping friends heartily on the backs as he accepted a glass of champagne. Alice was sure she saw him smile at Devon's departing back, an unkind, dismissive smile. Frowning, she turned away. Although she still felt envious of Leah's sponsorship deal, she was starting to realise it came at a price.

★

Later that evening Alice and Finn had managed to find some brilliant seats right by one of the huge Christmas-themed jumps, and they'd enjoyed a wonderful half-hour watching the big class, marvelling as the horses soared over the giant fence. Alice realised that she would be jumping in the same arena very soon. Although the jumps in her class on Sunday morning would be lower than those in the adult classes, the course would be just as technical. And she knew the designs would be just as extravagant: Christmas trees and giant candy canes. She couldn't wait!

But even though Alice was having a great time, she couldn't forget her conversation with Devon, and how it contrasted with Nick's story to the journalist. It was the way he'd referred to Talisman being sold... Of course, Nick had no doubt bought and sold a lot of ponies over the years but it didn't feel quite right, and it was playing on Alice's mind.

"You remember that girl at the Hyde Park stables." She turned to Finn in the interval. "Leah, with Kite? The sponsored one?"

"Mm." Finn was only half listening. "What about her?"

"Oh." Alice paused. "I don't know. Something doesn't seem right to me about the whole situation. Like, she can't have an opinion and is being controlled all the time. The owner – the sponsor guy – doesn't seem to care about the pony at all."

Finn glanced at her and gave a smile. "Alice," he said kindly, "why are you even worrying about her? You're jumping *against* this girl. She's got a super-rich company sponsoring her, and one of the best ponies in the country to ride. I mean, I think she's probably OK."

"Maybe." Alice said, but she remained unconvinced.

★

Alice was up extra early the next day. Her mum was driving down later and would leave the horsebox at the Hyde Park yard and then have dinner with some old school friends in the West End. Alice would head to Olympia and then they'd meet up afterwards to go back to the hotel they were going to be based in for the rest of their stay. Alice's Olympia moment with Secret was mere hours away now! She thought back to all her training with Angus, jumping round the local circuit, and although the nerves were peaking, so were her excitement levels.

When she got to the yard a short while later, bundled up against the cold in her thickest coat, Clare was just carrying out her first checks.

"Good morning!" she smiled. "I might see you later. I'm heading to Olympia with friends!"

Then she drew Alice aside. "Actually, Alice, I wondered if I could ask a favour?"

"OK," Alice replied, wondering what on earth she could help with.

"Kite hasn't really settled," Clare explained. "And sometimes a change of stables can help. As your pony seems such an easy chap, I wondered if you'd mind swapping stables just for the last night? I think Kite would be better in the big corner stable with a little more space."

"That's fine," Alice agreed. Secret was exceptionally easy-going, and he proved it by settling straight into his new stable, munching away at the hay net as if he had always been there. Kite seemed a little more relaxed too, and when Leah arrived a few moments later she was genuinely grateful.

"Thanks, Alice," she said. "I really appreciate it."

"It's no problem," Alice replied, and as the girls smiled at each other, Alice felt the tension of the last couple of days thaw a little. She remembered what Leah had said in the park during her disastrous photo shoot, how Kite just needed to hack out and take it easy before his big class. Suddenly she had an idea.

"Hey, do you want to ride out with me this morning?" she asked. "Only if you want to, or you don't have to be somewhere with your sponsors," she added hurriedly.

But Leah's smiled widened. "Yes please," she said softly. "I'd really like that."

It wasn't long before both girls were clattering out of the yard together, chatting away. Secret was thrilled to go out with Kite, who he'd taken a shine to, and as much as Alice had enjoyed the ride with Finn, it was nice to ride out with another girl the same age, with a shared interest in showjumping.

Leah seemed genuinely interested in Secret's history with Alice and their previous struggles, and then told Alice a little bit about her pony club.

"My parents aren't horsey in the slightest," Leah explained. "But when I was nine they managed to afford some lessons, and I started helping at the yard not long after that. Jackie, the lady who owns the stables, taught me to ride. She was really good to me and lent me her daughter's old pony, Bobby.

She took me to shows, and I joined the pony club attached to the stables. It was the best fun," she added, slightly wistfully, Alice thought.

"So how did the sponsorship deal come about?" Alice asked.

"Bobby was a brilliant showjumper and we had an inter-branch competition that I won," Leah replied. "Nick happened to be watching. He was looking for a keen rider they could sponsor up through the levels, but when I explained Bobby wasn't actually my pony, he told me about his plan to buy a pony from the Netherlands." She paused. "It was an amazing deal. My dad had just lost his job and I knew Mum and Dad wouldn't be able to afford my lessons for much longer. Jackie did try to convince me to stay with her." She paused, her voice wobbling a little. "But I couldn't carry on going to the shows, not being able to pay for entries and stuff. When Nick offered me the deal, it was like a lifeline. It came at just the right time." She leaned over and patted Kite. "And when I met Kite it was love at first sight. He's nervy and hot-headed but we just clicked; I understood him. I can't imagine anyone else riding him."

Alice felt a little humbled as she listened. She loved ponies more than anything. They were all she thought about at school; all she wanted to do at the weekends. But she'd never been in a situation where she couldn't actually ride a pony. Even when she'd given up for a while, after her first pony, Honey, had died, horses were still a huge part of family life. And Leah obviously loved ponies as much as she did.

"How long have you been sponsored?" she asked.

"About eighteen months," Leah explained. "Kite was bred in the Netherlands, and when he came over here I thought I would have three or four years to get him to the level he is at now. He's hard work, really sensitive, and it doesn't take a lot to upset him. Even going away overnight can wind him up. But Nick threw everything at us, the best trainers, entries to the big qualifiers." She frowned. "If Kite was my very own pony, I would have taken it slower. I mean, he's coped so far, he's super-talented and everything but … sometimes it's just a bit much, you know? He really needs to just chill out for a bit. Look at your pony, super-relaxed. Kite's never like that."

Alice thought carefully about what she was going to say. "Surely if Kite has been given to you to ride, you're allowed a say in what happens with him?"

But Leah shook her head. "I wish," she sighed. "If he could have a break and just do some lower-level stuff for a while, I think that would really help him." She chewed on her lip. "I blame myself a bit. I've been too scared to say anything to Nick. Kite's not ready for Sunday, not the way he is at the moment."

Alice looked at the handsome skewbald, who still looked unsettled. She knew Secret could be cheeky and exuberant, but it was always with a joyful demeanour. Kite just seemed stressed, no matter how quietly Leah was riding him.

"Well, why don't you say something now?" Alice said, thinking of Nick. He didn't seem like a nice person, but surely he wouldn't want to risk stressing and potentially ruining his star pony.

"He's already hinted I'm being a nuisance by even questioning him," Leah said, sounding miserable. "You have to remember, he's not my pony. Nick's invested big money in Kite and he wants results. They've got a big deal going on at the moment and he needs an Olympia placing to boost the profile of Hadley." She hesitated. "I overheard him telling someone – boasting, really – that Kite is insured for over one hundred thousand pounds."

Alice's mouth fell open. That was an eye-wateringly huge amount of money for a young pony.

"But truthfully," Leah continued, "he's not that interested in Kite. He never pats him, he barely looks at him really. He's only interested in what he can do for his company. And as Nick often reminds me, there's always a rider behind me, ready to take my place. Horse-mad girls who can ride a bit and can't afford a pony are as common as anything, he says." She paused. "So I haven't spoken out before, but I know I need to now."

Chapter 10

The girls had ridden on in companionable silence, Alice thinking about Leah's words. It seemed the expensive wool rugs, photo shoots and branded kit were not all they were cracked up to be if they came with the control Nick exerted over Leah and Kite – the constant threat of having her pony taken away and given to someone else to ride. She thought again of Devon, but decided against mentioning the showjumper to Leah, after her reaction last time.

"That was really nice," Leah smiled as they untacked their ponies side by side back at the yard. "Thank you." She paused. "It's been ages since I rode out with anyone. When I rode with Jackie, I had loads of friends I could ride with, but you know…" Her voice tailed off and she shook her head.

Alice was still thinking about Leah's words as she cleaned her tack in the heated tack room later. She still couldn't get over the fact Kite was worth over one hundred thousand pounds. For a pony who'd only been on the competition circuit for a short amount of time!

Her thoughts were interrupted by raised voices outside. Peering out at the smart arena, Alice watched Kite cantering around, before Leah aimed him at a jump. Kite was clearly on edge and not seeming to focus at all on the simple straight bar. It was different from Secret, who bounded gleefully into the fences.

To Alice's surprise Kite refused the jump, but she was impressed with the way Leah sat quietly and didn't once pick up her whip, instead giving him a quick pat before circling and attempting the jump again. Kite gave a high-pitched whinny and Alice could see Leah was struggling to get the pony to concentrate. They cleared the fence the second time but it was obvious Kite wasn't in the zone. Leah patted him, pulling him up next to a man Alice hadn't seen before, dressed in smart breeches. He exchanged a few words with Leah, nodded and then turned to Nick, who was clearly furious.

Edging closer, Alice tried to work out what was being said.

"I agree with Leah." The man in breeches had

a calm air about him, in stark contrast to Nick. "It's been too much this year. Kite's barely had a moment's rest and I think Olympia is a step too far."

"But he qualified!" Nick said angrily. "He's perfectly capable."

The man in breeches shook his head. "Qualifying is one thing, actually competing at Olympia quite another. There's always next year, even the year after," he said. Leah looked grateful for the back-up. "Why push him too hard? He'll just burn out. He's not the easiest pony, you know that."

"With all due respect," Nick practically spat, "he's *my* pony. I pay you to get the ponies to the top, not go all soft on me."

"It's too much," Leah said firmly, her voice strong. She was finally speaking out, Alice realised, feeling proud of her. "You can see for yourself he's wound up and his jumping is suffering.

I don't think he'll do well at all. I told you, he needs a couple of months in the field to chill him out." She paused, and it seemed her resolve was strengthening. "I'm not jumping him, and that's that."

Nick glared at her. "We'll talk about this later, *Leah*."

Leah didn't say anything, but her face fell. Alice remembered her words, how it would break her heart to lose the ride on Kite. But Nick couldn't take away her ride, just for trying to do the right thing … could he?

"I might see you later?" Leah popped her head round the door. She'd changed into jeans and her scarlet-branded jacket, her auburn hair tied neatly into a long plait. Her face gave away none of her emotions. "At Olympia, I mean."

"Yes," Alice smiled. "I'm going for the evening

performance." And then as Leah was still hovering in the doorway, she added. "Shall we meet up? We could watch some of the show together? My friend Finn is riding."

And just like when Alice had invited Leah riding, Leah relaxed into a smile.

"Yes, please," she said. "I have to go on the stand first, then I'm free."

After exchanging telephone numbers, Leah was off. Alice smiled, resuming her tack cleaning. She hoped for Leah's sake it would all work out for her, withdrawing Kite from his class. Perhaps Nick would understand once he'd had a chance to cool down a bit. She knew from experience the worst thing you could do was push a pony before it was ready, or didn't want to do what it was you were competing in. She'd learned that the hard way with Secret in the show ring. And Leah had the back-up of the obviously experienced instructor.

As Alice ran a damp sponge over the soft leather she thought back to how envious she'd been of Leah. Not any more. At least Alice would always have a say in what she did with Secret!

★

Alice had a routine now: the bus journey, the fastest way round to the backstage area, and who was who in each of the stables. Watching a Whitaker sail over the most enormous practice fence, she did have to pause for just a moment, allowing it to wash over her. Being backstage had been brilliant. She'd been able to get right up to her favourite horsey heroes and watch how they did things, and meeting Devon was the highlight.

As she passed the Hadley Feeds trade stand, she noticed a huge, life-size cardboard cut-out of Leah and Kite sailing over a fence.

Nick was standing at the front, chatting animatedly with a small group of people, champagne glass in hand. Any trace of his anger from earlier was gone as he laughed and joked loudly. Leah was being completely ignored and Alice wondered what she was meant to be doing. Held up by the dawdlers in front of her admiring a crystal-studded saddlecloth on the stand next door, Alice watched as a girl about her own age approached Nick in a confident manner. She hovered next to him for a minute before Nick turned to her with a pleasant smile.

"Can I help you?"

The girl launched into what sounded like a sales pitch. From the bits Alice could hear, she had a loan pony that was being sold and her parents couldn't afford to buy him.

"But we're doing so well," the girl said passionately. "We were class winners at the local county show and we've been in the pony club team for the last two years. Would you consider sponsoring me, one day?"

And she pulled out her phone, presumably to show Nick footage of her riding.

"See, that's me winning the junior open," the girl explained. "And that's me at areas, and that's—"

Nick handed the phone back.

"Lovely," he said in a charming voice. "I'll take your details and perhaps I'll come and watch a class. I'm always looking for new opportunities."

Then he flashed the quickest glance at Leah.

"You might hear from me sooner than you think."

And after he'd taken the girl's name and number and given her one of his cards, she skipped off with her friends, clearly delighted.

Ugh, Alice thought. She bet the girl wouldn't have approached Nick if she knew what he'd been like with Leah earlier. Then Alice remembered that only a couple of days ago she herself had been green with envy over Leah's gorgeous rugs and coats and sponsorship too.

Catching Leah's eye, Alice gave a small wave and Leah gestured for Alice to join her. Seizing the opportunity, Alice sneaked in round the side to say hello.

"All OK?"

Leah rolled her eyes. "Seems I'm not too popular right now," she said in a low voice. "Nick agreed we can withdraw Kite but he cancelled the meet and greet. Only he didn't tell me, so it's all a bit awkward."

"Oh," Alice said. "But that's good he agreed you can withdraw, if you're sure?"

Leah nodded. "One hundred per cent," she said. "I know Kite wouldn't have coped with the atmosphere. He wouldn't have performed well. He needs to mature a bit more. And Nick was actually OK about it in the end, so that's good.

He's arranged for a lorry to come and get him. I can go home with him tomorrow."

Alice smiled. She thought fondly of her own little gelding tucked up safely in his stable, who'd never minded an overnight stay away and who loved an audience. In fact, the bigger the crowd, the better the performance!

"But even though I'm sad not to be jumping now," Leah continued, "it's been a nice week. Thanks so much," she said a little awkwardly. "For inviting me riding, and hanging out and stuff." She smiled. "Sorry I was so spiky when we met."

"It's fine," Alice said. "Really. It's been good to have someone to hang out with." She thought of Finn, who was so busy with the Rebel Riders, now doing some sort of promo thing for the camera crews. Their lives were so different these days, so it was good to have a new friend by her side.

★

"Leah, this is Finn," she said, as Finn rode up on Horatio a bit later. In his blue jacket and with his black hair tousled, Alice couldn't stop her tummy flipping over. She'd noticed that Finn was attracting quite a bit of attention, and earlier in the week had even signed some autographs for girls who grinned up at him, tossing their hair over shoulders, practically elbowing Alice out of the way!

Leah and Finn shook hands politely, before Finn headed off to get ready for his entrance with the Rebel Riders.

Leah turned to Alice, a glint in her eye. "Um, hello?!" she said. "He's pretty gorgeous, isn't he? Is he your boyfriend?"

Alice blushed and told Leah about how she and Finn had become close. It was actually really nice to have Leah to chat to. She'd never told anyone at school about Finn, and it could be a bit awkward at pony club with Angus working there!

Then they watched the display together, clapping and cheering throughout.

"OK, my week has got even better now," Leah grinned as the Rebel Riders galloped off to thunderous applause. "That's seriously cool!"

Later on Alice went to get a hot chocolate for herself, Finn and Leah, and found herself standing behind Nick and another man in the queue at one of the coffee stands. Nick's earlier charm from the trade stand was gone, replaced with a cold tone as he talked to the man next to him.

"Is the trade lorry still leaving Golden Fields?" he said, his voice soft but somehow menacing.

The man nodded. "As discussed, boss. Two containers. They've already been dropped off."

"Well, tell them to wait," Nick continued. "I want to add another container. Something last minute, you get what I mean?"

"Sure," the man replied. "I can get one of the boys on it if you give me the pick-up location. Is it a Talisman scenari—"

But he was interrupted as a woman glided up, a member's badge dangling from her expensive-looking handbag.

"Nick!" she cried. "Great to see you." And in an instant, the smooth grin was back on Nick's face as he air-kissed the woman on both cheeks, proclaiming loudly how wonderful it was to see her and how great she looked.

Alice paid for her hot chocolates, frowning as she watched Nick and his associate leave with the lady. She knew Hadley distributed high-end horse feed all over Europe, but what was the reference to Talisman? She thought of Kite, going home tomorrow, and hoped Leah would be OK.

Then she shook herself, remembering Finn's words. She was jumping on Sunday and then she and Leah would go back to their own lives and their paths wouldn't cross again. She just had to focus on herself and Secret!

★

During the interval, Alice had an urge to go and see her pony rather than watch the second half of the show. It had been a long day and she just wanted to have a few moments with Secret in his stable. She had plenty of time to get back to Olympia afterwards to meet her mum. She told Leah her plan, who smiled.

"Good idea," she said. "Can I come with you?"

Alice nodded happily and then texted her mum, who replied quickly.

No problem, the message read. *As long as you're with your friend. Just about to go into the restaurant now, love you!*

And Alice smiled, glad her mum was having a rare night off.

The two girls chatted companionably as they made the short journey by bus, hopping off outside the stables.

Kite popped his handsome conker head over his door, uttering a low, rumbly whinny as he caught sight of Leah.

"Hello, boy," Leah said softly, and Alice smiled. The affection between the pair was only too obvious. She was glad she'd been able to help in a small way, swapping stables to help the nervy gelding relax.

Secret was probably flat out, snoozing in his shavings bed, Alice thought fondly as she approached his stable. But then she felt a wave of confusion as she noticed that although the stable door remained closed, the special clip she'd brought from home to stop Secret escaping was lying discarded on the cobbles. Surely Secret hadn't learned how to get that off?

"Secret?" she said, awaiting the familiar whicker and sounds of hooves on concrete as he scrabbled up to see her, flecked with shavings. "What have you been up to?"

But then she neared the stable and her heart stopped.

Secret was gone.

Chapter 11

For a moment time stood still as the rational part of Alice's brain tried to reason with her thudding heart. Looking again, she scanned every part of the stable, desperately hoping her eyes were playing tricks and Secret had tucked himself into a corner. Then she took a deep breath. It was Secret! Of course, he would have just got out and would be making friends somewhere in another part of the yard. She tried to ignore the fact that his stable door had been bolted neatly behind him.

"Leah?" she called, her voice higher than normal. "It's Secret. He's not here!"

Looking confused, Leah gave Kite a pat and came to join her.

"What do you mean?"

"I think he's got out," Alice said, trying to quell the rising panic that told her it was more than that. "You look left, I'll look right."

Racing around the yard, peering down every walkway and behind every block of stables, the panic started to rise further, blocking her throat and crushing her chest as horses blinked sleepily at Alice, disturbed by her running. Then she looked up as a man came through the gates, whistling a cheery tune that seemed quite at odds with the fear she felt.

"Hello," the man smiled. "I'm Gareth. I help

Clare from time to time when she's away. You must be Alice and Leah, am I right?"

Then he frowned, noticing Alice's white face. Alice was trying to stop a sob escaping. What if Secret was out on the roads? But the stable door had been bolted. She knew that he hadn't escaped. Something else was going on.

"My pony, Secret." Her voice came out in ragged gasps. "He's been taken!"

Gareth looked confused. "No," he said. "Secret's still here. Only one pony has gone tonight. I signed him out. Kite B?"

Alice and Leah stared at each other, desperately trying to work out what was going on.

"Kite's still here," Leah said in a trembling voice.

Gareth started to look worried. "Hang on," he said, as if trying to make sense of everything. "Clare asked me to come in and do the feeds while she was at Olympia. She said Kite's owners were visiting, so when they took him out I assumed they'd already agreed that with Clare."

"He's meant to be going home tomorrow," Leah said. "With *me*. What's going on?"

Alice shook her head. "Kite's owner, Nick, was at Olympia earlier this evening," she said to Gareth. "What did the person look like?"

Gareth frowned deeply. "He was tall with blond hair, drove a white horsebox," he said. "He had all the paperwork … everything. He had a lanyard with his name on from Hadley Feeds. Nick."

Alice shook her head, feeling like she might be sick.

"That's not Nick," she whispered. "And why have they taken my Secret?"

Leah had grown even whiter, her hands trembling as she placed a hand on Alice's arm.

"Alice," she said in a horrified voice. "That man was meant to take Kite, Nick must have sent him.

And he's taken the wrong pony!"

★

The first person Alice called was her mum, but there was no answer and despite calling seven times, it went to voicemail.

"Mum, call me!" Alice left a message in a shaky voice.

With nothing to suggest where Secret had been taken, Alice and Leah caught the nearest taxi back to Olympia to see Finn.

Barely able to sit still, her legs drumming up and down as she willed the cab to get to Olympia as fast as it could, Alice's brain was in overdrive. She thought of the little red gelding boarding a strange lorry. He'd be looking around for her. Sometimes he stopped at the bottom of the ramp, just to sniff it, but what if that made whoever was loading him impatient and cross? What if they hit him, to move him up the ramp faster? He always got a mint when he was tied up, but no one would have given him one tonight. He'd be so confused, Alice thought, fear rising in her. She thought about the stable swap earlier in the day; sweet, trusting Secret, who'd saved the day and allowed Kite to settle a bit. And had unwittingly been placed right into the heart of danger.

Then she frowned as she remembered The Talisman, and the mistake Nick had made about his fate when he was talking to the journalist ... then the way the other man had mentioned him in the coffee queue. What *was* supposed to happen to Kite? Why had Nick arranged for him to be picked up earlier? And now, what would happen to Secret, taken by mistake? All Alice knew was that she had to find him, and fast!

Her thoughts were interrupted by the sound of sniffing, and, looking over, Alice could see Leah crying.

"I'm sorry," was all she would say.

"It's not your fault." Alice meant it. How was Leah to know?

"Maybe not," Leah said quietly. "But," she looked up at Alice, "truthfully, I thought something was up. But Nick ... Nick..." Her voice trailed off.

"Nick what?" Alice said impatiently.

"He told me to keep out of it, if I knew what was good for me." Leah's voice was barely a whisper, and an icy hand gripped Alice's spine.

"There were just things I noticed," Leah continued, face downcast as Alice listened intently. "Like he arranged for a vetting to be done last week, but it wasn't the vet I normally saw, and Nick told me not to mention it to anyone. He just said that the insurers had asked for another opinion." She paused. "Remember when I said how scared I was about losing my ride on Kite?" Alice nodded. "I'd have done anything to keep him, but things have felt wrong recently. I should have insisted he be withdrawn much earlier. Then Secret would be safe. It's all my fault." And she started to cry.

"Leah," Alice said, almost fiercely. "You have to stay strong. I need your help finding my pony!"

After quickly finding Finn, the friends set off in search of Nick.

"It might just be an honest mistake," reassured Finn. "He has to know what's going on."

With Finn and Leah in hot pursuit Alice raced out into the trade-stand area, heading straight for the scarlet and gold stall. A girl in her early twenties was just packing up.

"That's Jen," Leah said to Alice as they approached. "Nick's assistant."

"Hey." Jen gave a start as she saw Leah. "I thought you'd gone home already? Nick said he'd pulled you out of the competition because you no longer wanted to ride Kite. Everyone's been talking about it..." Her voice trailed off as she looked at Leah's face. "Is everything OK?"

"Jen, do you know where Nick is?" Leah said urgently, obviously shocked by what Jen had said about her not wanting to ride Kite. *More twisting of the truth,* Alice thought.

Jen looked genuinely confused. "What?" she said. "No I don't, sorry. He said something about going out for dinner somewhere with some investors, but he left in a bit of a hurry."

"OK." Alice took a deep breath. Her mind was whirring, sharpening things into focus. "Let's think about why Nick would have taken Kite away early. Then maybe we can find Secret."

"Why don't we just ring him?" Finn said, looking perplexed. "Surely it's just a mix-up? Maybe the transporter just changed the time he was being taken home?"

But Alice shook her head. "No," she said. "That

will only alert him to the fact we know something. I'm *sure* something dodgy is going on. I just don't know what."

Just then Devon appeared by the stand.

"Alice?" Devon's normally smiley face was concerned as she placed a hand on Alice's arm. "I heard something had happened with the Hadley Feeds pony."

Alice shook her head. "It was supposed to be Kite, but Secret was taken instead."

"But Kite is a completely different colour, isn't he?" Devon frowned, and Alice nodded.

"Whoever took him wasn't Nick. The description didn't fit," she explained. "I'm guessing they were told to take the pony in stable two – and didn't know what they were meant to be taking. Both ponies were in hoods… It was dark…"

Seeing Devon again was making Alice's head spin. She was *sure* that there was a connection between what had happened to The Talisman and what was planned for Kite. There were just too many similarities!

"Devon." She turned the older girl. "Do you remember who took The Talisman home from his last competition?"

Devon frowned. "The same transporters who always took him everywhere," she said. "A man called Charlie."

"Did you ever ask him for *his* version about what happened?" Alice pressed.

Devon shook her head. "No," she said. "I didn't. Nick just shut me out. 'He's dead, that's all you need to know,' he told me." She paused. "All I had was the mane cutting and the vet's report on his injuries. Nick didn't even tell me where he'd been cremated. Tally was just an asset to him, nothing more."

"Could we contact Charlie?" Alice asked,

desperately clutching at straws.

"I have a number," Devon said, biting her lip. "But I don't know if it still works. It's been six years."

"Please try," Alice pleaded. This could be their one lead.

Nodding, Devon pulled out her phone and scrolled through it, before putting the phone hesitantly to her ear.

Alice, Finn and Leah held their breath collectively as Devon spoke.

"Charlie?" she said, her voice nervous. "It's Devon Jenkins." She gave a small smile, seeming to relax. "I know, it's been too long. Thank you, yes, the horses are going great. Listen, this is going to sound strange but I wanted to ask you something … about what happened six years ago."

Alice paced up and down as Devon looked serious, nodding at various intervals as she listened. Alice just wanted to run, to run round the whole of the city until she found her beloved pony.

"OK," Devon finally said, her voice quiet. "Thanks so much, Charlie. I appreciate it."

Hanging up, she turned to Alice. The older girl's eyes were filled with tears, but she had a quiet anger about her.

"Charlie told me that he dropped Tally off at a pick-up point," she said. "He was told Nick would take him on, with me, for some extra training at a jumping yard. Charlie told me Tally was fine, that he hadn't suffered any injury with him, so it must have been when he was with Nick. But Nick said Tally had been injured in *Charlie's* box. He never said anything about swapping horseboxes." She put a hand on her forehead and closed her eyes. "I was just too upset, knowing he'd died. *Why* didn't I ask more questions at the time?" she said, almost to herself.

"Does Charlie remember anything about where he dropped him off?" Finn asked, and Devon frowned.

"No," she said. "Only that it was somewhere in south London. It was just some random drop-off point with a few stables, he said. But he does remember Nick having a white horsebox, and he thought it was odd because he'd always hired Charlie to take Tally to the shows. So why would he suddenly need a horsebox?"

Alice and Leah exchanged glances. Gareth at the Hyde Park yard had mentioned a white horsebox. But that was all they had. Secret could be heading anywhere in the country. Groaning, she slumped back, before feeling Finn's hand on her arm, steadying her.

"Alice," he said, and Alice tried to focus on her friend. He drew her close.

"This is Secret. We'll find him, we will."

But Alice could hear the worry in his voice. She had to believe his words. She wasn't going to let herself think of the alternative. Not yet.

Chapter 12

The minutes were ticking by fast and Alice felt as if she was wading in treacle, unsure where to turn, her mind heavy with worry. What would Nick do when he realised he had the wrong pony? Alice shuddered, wishing she hadn't thought about that.

Then she sat up straight, thinking back to what Leah had said in the stables after they rode together. Kite was worth a huge amount of money; he was an incredibly valuable asset to Nick. But what if that was exactly how he viewed him? As no more than an asset, just as Devon had said he saw Talisman. Tally had been worth a similar amount. Leah said he barely looked at Kite, much less showed any sort of affection for him. Her thoughts were interrupted by Jen, who was walking over, clutching something.

"Leah?" she said, her voice quiet and urgent. "Leah, I just found this in Nick's handwriting. He must have dropped it." And she handed over a crumpled receipt for two coffees with scrawled writing on the back. Leah read it, a frown deepening.

"Meet @ GF ind estate 10pm," Leah read aloud, her face pale. "What does this mean?"

"I've no idea," Jen shrugged.

"OK," Devon said. "What time did he leave tonight?"

Jen looked thoughtful. "About an hour ago, I guess."

Alice's mind was whirring now, trying to work out timings. It was nearly nine thirty. Nick was meeting someone very soon at *GF ind estate…* Suddenly, she had it.

"GF … Golden Fields!" she blurted out, and everyone turned to her, looking confused.

"Golden Fields?" Jen said. "Hadley used to have a depot there, years ago. Nick used to send big loads of horse feed abroad from there. I once saw it on some old invoices when I was doing the accounts."

Finn was already tapping his phone, squinting at the screen.

"Golden Fields, Golden Fields," he muttered, and then his eyes lit up. "Aha!" he said triumphantly.

"Golden Fields Industrial Estate, SE26."

"It's not a yard though," Leah said doubtfully. "Why would they take a pony there?"

"But it *is* about an hour away, according to the map," Finn continued, looking up from the screen. "What do you think?"

Alice took a deep breath. They had no leads, apart from the name, and no sightings, apart from the horsebox. But they had to try, if there was any chance that Secret had been taken there. A shiver went through Alice as she thought about Nick's words. He had wanted to add another container. Now she was sure that the extra container was a pony. Kite – and now Secret. She nodded.

"We have to go there," she said firmly.

But Leah looked worried. "I don't know," she said. "And I'm scared about Kite. What if… What if when Nick realises the wrong pony has been taken they go back for him?"

Alice paused. In all the worry with Secret going missing she'd totally forgotten about the original intended victim.

"I'll stay with him," Devon said, and they all turned to her. She had a look of determination on her face. "If it helps to keep him safe and we can work out what happened with Tally and Secret, then I'll guard him."

Leah nodded. "Thank you," she said gratefully, scribbling down the yard address and gate codes.

"I think you should call the police too," Devon said.

With shaky hands, Alice dialled the emergency number.

"A pony, missing?" the operator repeated back to her.

"Yes," she said desperately. "He's been kidnapped, only it's a case of mistaken identity."

"Look," the operator sighed. "As you can

imagine, this side of Christmas we are extremely busy. I'll open a case number, but—"

Then Alice remembered something. The mounted police.

"Wait!" she cried. "Can you at least see if you can pass a message on?" She tried desperately to remember the names. "Officer Edward … Hill, yes that's it! Officer Hill! And Fairbanks, Officer Fairbanks. They ride police horses. Please can you tell them it's Alice, with Secret the roan pony, and that I think Nick from Hadley Feeds is up to no good. We're going to the Golden Fields Industrial Estate. Please tell them!"

"OK." The operator sounded unconvinced and Alice could hear the tap of her keyboard as she made notes. "I'll do my best to pass that on."

"Right," Finn put his arm around Alice. "Let's go."

And with her two friends either side of her, Alice

felt a wave of relief. Having them with her meant she felt a little less afraid.

★

Devon was the first to leave – hailing a cab to take her to Hyde Park stables. It was a clear, freezing night, and as Alice looked up at the sky she had a sudden longing to be in the yard at home, where the air was clear and fresh, with Secret tucked up in his own stable. She partly blamed herself; that's where he *should* have been tonight, but she'd been so eager to take advantage of the backstage ticket that she'd moved him right into the path of danger. Then she shook herself. Secret had been in a lovely, safe yard in London, and they'd had two brilliant rides around Hyde Park. She hadn't known what was going to happen.

It suddenly occurred to her that they had just hours to check Secret into his stable at Olympia and declare herself as a competitor in the Pony

Club class, the class she'd been dreaming about for months, all the hard work leading up to that three-minute turn in the arena. None of it seemed to matter right now though; she just wanted Secret home and safe.

The next cab they flagged down was driven by a jolly-looking man who frowned slightly as Alice recited the address to him.

"It's a long way out," he said doubtfully, looking at the group with a little suspicion. Alice realised they looked slightly odd, her and Leah in their normal jeans and Finn still in the blue and gold military jacket and breeches, with golden-green make-up smudged around his dark eyes.

"I'm sorry," she said. "But we really, *really* need to get there, and fast!"

Shrugging, the taxi driver put his cab into gear and headed down the high street, the twinkle of the Christmas lights in every shop window providing false cheer as Alice sat as far forward in her seat as she could, willing the car to move through the city traffic as quickly as possible. No one really spoke, but sensing Leah's fear, Alice took her hand.

"Remember what I said back there," Alice said quietly. "It's not your fault. If it wasn't Secret, it would have been Kite."

Leah nodded, biting her lip. Alice turned away from her and watched the city crawl past the window. The bright lights of the high street gradually merged into office blocks and suburban housing, then industrial estates with smoke pouring from chimneys. Finn reached over and took Alice's other hand, and she squeezed it gratefully, glad he was with her. The driver cleared his throat.

"Coming up to it." He threw a concerned glance in their direction as he flicked on the indicators. "Are you sure this is the place you want?"

Alice stared upwards at the imposing walls, clad in blocks of varying greys. There was an air of dinginess and the place was deserted, unlike the other industrial estates they'd passed on their way. But the peeling plastic sign by the big steel gates read "Golden Fields". *Secret might be within those walls,* she thought. They had to do all they could to find him.

"We're sure," she said firmly, and after pooling their money to pay the driver, the three teenagers were alone on the pavement outside.

The gates were already open so they crept through, sticking close to each other, their shadows long in the faint orange glow of lights from neighbouring buildings. The continuous hum of traffic on the ring road above them provided background noise, but it felt as though all Alice could hear was the beating of her own heart as they crossed the large expanse of concrete. She bit her lip. It seemed so unlikely her pony was going to be here. What if it was too late? Nick was obviously sending the lorry somewhere, but where? Alice couldn't bear to think about it. Secret was the other half of her, her very best friend.

"Wait," Finn suddenly said, and everyone paused.

Alice held her breath. Up ahead of them was the faintest glow of lights, as if something was behind the buildings. Alice's stomach turned over as her ears caught the smallest of sounds, a sound she knew so well, a sound so out of place here.

Hooves on concrete.

Secret!

Chapter 13

"Alice," Finn called warningly, trying to pull her back, but it was too late. Alice had sprinted forward towards the faint lights, running down an alleyway between the dingy buildings, aware of Leah and Finn behind her.

Stopping dead, she found herself in the glare of headlights, which momentarily blinded her. An enormous lorry was parked up behind the estate, and she could just make out the outline of two men standing beside it, deep in angry conversation. One was gesticulating wildly to the other, and voices were raised. Abruptly, the shorter of the men turned, and Alice swallowed hard, suddenly aware they'd run right into the path of danger. Looking wildly around, she then realised with horror that she was all alone. Where were the others?

"Get off me!" she heard Leah cry out, and with a cold stab of dread realised there were probably more than two men.

The shorter man took a step towards her, his hands clenched in fists.

"Who are you?"

It was Nick, and his tone was menacing, quiet. Alice stood her ground.

"You have my pony and I want him back," she said, in a shaky voice that she hoped didn't betray the fear she felt.

"I don't know what you're talking about, little girl," Nick spat, taking another step forward. "You'd better clear off right now, do you hear me?"

In a split second he'd lunged at her arm, fleshy fingers just grazing her elbow. But Alice was too quick. She might not be the best at running, but fear made her fast and she sprinted down the side of the lorry, before realising she was trapped. Thinking quickly as Nick and the other man caught up with her, she tucked herself into a roll, diving under the lowered ramp of the lorry. Climbing out from the other side, she felt her heart lift with relief as a pony trotted into view, silhouetted against the lights. Secret!

But a groan escaped her lips as the pony neared. Bigger than Secret, the pony was a gorgeous grey mare, who fleetingly reminded Alice of Ella. The pony seemed nervous, and paused, ears on high alert, whole body quivering.

"Get the blasted pony!" she heard Nick yell, and she saw him, red-faced, clambering over the ramp. On she ran. Secret had to be here; where else could he be? Then, rounding a corner, she stopped dead, the sight in front of her making her want to laugh out loud in sheer delight.

There was a little red pony with a stable bolt between his lips, easing the metal back until the door on a ramshackle wooden stable sprang back and the clearly panicked bay pony inside cantered out, hooves scrabbling on the concrete.

"Secret!"

Hearing her voice Secret lifted his head, his whole body seeming to tremble as he searched out Alice in the darkness.

"Oh, Secret!" Alice started to run towards him, then gave a cry of horror as another man appeared from nowhere, flinging a rope around Secret's neck. Secret had been so focused on getting to Alice he hadn't noticed the man, but now he was caught.

Rage took over Alice, totally eclipsing any fear she felt. Lunging forward, she grabbed the man's arm, clawing and hitting, anything to make him let go of Secret. Then she turned and watched in horror as the lorry moved forward, and the men attempted to round up the grey mare and the bay pony Secret had released.

"That blasted roan!" she heard one of the men swear. "If he hadn't let these two out they'd be on the lorry by now!"

And despite the circumstances, Alice felt like cheering. Hooray for her brave pony, whose escaping tricks at home both exasperated and amused her, and now, by the sounds of it, had delayed any plans to leave the estate.

"It doesn't matter about him," she heard Nick hiss. "Just get these two on board!"

"You won't get away with this!" Alice shouted at Nick as he approached. She was still trying to claw the rope back from the man who had hold of Secret. Nick seemed to look through her, and with a cry of horror Alice realised the terrified ponies had been loaded on to the box, forced up the ramp that had been purposely backed into the corner to allow the ponies no escape.

Using all her strength, she tried once again to wrench the rope free, just as Secret took matters into his own hands. Alice had always prided herself on the fact Secret didn't bite or kick, apart from the time he'd nipped Seb in France. But frightened by the shouting and Alice's distress, Secret whipped his head round and bit the man very hard on his upper arm. The man screeched and dropped the rope immediately, pulling up his sleeve to reveal deep teeth marks. It was only a few seconds' grace but it was enough for Alice to vault up on to Secret's back and wheel him around, back towards the main gates.

"Alice!"

Finn! Thank goodness he was safe. Alice turned to see him running towards her with Leah. He was about fifty metres from the entrance.

"We've got to stop that lorry leaving!" she shouted as Secret clattered over the concrete.

Looking behind, seeing the headlights illuminated, Finn nodded.

"OK!" he yelled, and he and Leah sprinted back.

Alice could see they were making a real effort to try and push one of the big steel-clad gates forward, their shoes slipping on the concrete as they edged it shut. Slowly, slowly, they were closing the gap.

Alice had nearly reached the gates now, ready

to leap off and help her friends shut the lorry in. The huge vehicle was descending on them though, revving hard.

"Come on, boy!" she urged Secret on, and then out of nowhere another man appeared, lunging at them. Swerving to the side, Secret spun round and Alice had no chance. She grabbed a handful of red mane but met only air as she clattered down on to the concrete, knocking every breath out of her body and hitting her head hard.

Secret was out of reach; he was safe, she thought desperately as she felt Finn kneel beside her and heard the lorry pull around them. But Nick had the other ponies. Alice's head was spinning and she thought she might be sick, but just as the lorry turned out of the gates a blur of blue lights appeared in front of her eyes. The wail of sirens grew closer until suddenly three police cars screeched to a halt and the big lorry was blocked in. Aware that Finn had pulled her close, Alice's only thought was Secret. She just wanted to be with him, but her head was hurting too much to think now. And then, everything went black.

Chapter 14

"Alice!"

The voice calling her name seemed very far away. Alice tried to force her eyes open.

"Alice, you're OK." The voice was familiar; she felt safe. "Look, the ambulance is here now."

Alice was aware of someone else crouching besides her, of murmured words.

"Secret…" She tried to talk, but words seemed

hard to find; her tongue felt too big for her mouth. There was a strange metallic taste, and wiping her sleeve against her lip, she frowned at the red stain on her coat.

"Secret's safe." It was Finn talking, and as Alice glanced up she saw her beloved red pony standing beside Leah, shifting restlessly from foot to foot.

"Kite," she croaked, remembering Devon. "Is Kite safe?"

"We've checked. He's safe too." Another voice, one Alice recognised from her happy ride around Hyde Park. Officer Rosie Fairbanks knelt beside her. "We got your message and came as soon as we could."

Alice looked up. The lorry was parked and two ponies, one bay and one grey, stood beside it, police officers clutching lead ropes. She felt a wave of relief.

"And Nick?" she stammered.

Officer Fairbanks gave a grim smile.

"We've got him," she said. "At last."

★

Alice had insisted she was fine, but trying to stand up she suddenly felt very wobbly, the pain in her head increasing.

"I want Mum," was all she could manage, and Rosie bent down, smiling kindly.

"We'll ring her," she reassured her. "We'll need to get your pony safely back to Hyde Park while you're checked over in hospital."

Hospital!

Alice shook her head. Now she'd found Secret, there was no way she was leaving his side.

"No," she croaked. "I'm OK, really..."

The paramedics who were tending her swam into focus. One raised an eyebrow, his smile kind but firm.

"Absolutely no arguments, young lady," he

said. "You need to come in."

Looking desperately at Finn, Alice relaxed slightly to see him holding Secret. The little gelding adored Finn, and Alice knew she could trust him to keep her beloved pony safe. But something was wrong. Secret was dancing around, pulling the rope from Finn's hands as he tried to keep him steady. The normally confident pony was showing real fear in his eyes, desperately calling to Alice as she was loaded on to a stretcher.

"Secret." Alice tried to call to him but her voice was barely a whisper. "Secret, I'll be back for you, I promise."

But Secret was clearly panicked, plunging around, half rearing as he tried to escape Finn's grip and get to Alice as she was carried into the waiting ambulance.

"Make sure he's OK," she pleaded with Leah. The little red pony whinnied over and over, his cries cutting through the night.

"You know we will," Leah said, but her voice betrayed her worry as Secret reared again, higher this time, almost knocking Finn to the floor. As Alice was lifted into the back of the ambulance and the doors closed behind her all she saw was the look in Secret's eyes, and it haunted her.

Alice hadn't been in an ambulance since the awful day her pony Honey had died, collapsing while cross-country jumping, and severely injuring Alice in the process. Suddenly the lights and machine beeps seemed horribly familiar, and, without realising it, she reached up to the faint scar on her cheek, the only physical reminder of that day. She'd vowed to never love another pony … until Secret had come into her life. And she'd so nearly lost him tonight. The glory of the Olympia ring faded away. All that mattered was Secret.

★

Alice wasn't sure how long it had taken to get into hospital. She'd been whisked in and seen straight away for a scan, but she was feeling better all the time. She was diagnosed with mild concussion, but, as the smiling doctor had said, she'd been extremely lucky.

"Every time we get a horsey person in, I marvel at their toughness," he'd told her. "And I bet all you want to do is get back to your pony, am I right?"

And Alice had nodded. That was *exactly* what she wanted to do. Her phone screen had been smashed in the fall but she could just make out a text from Finn, reassuring her that Secret had arrived safely back at Hyde Park.

But then, hearing a familiar voice, she felt herself crumble.

"My daughter, Alice Smalley." Josephine

sounded frightened. "Thank you."

Pulling aside the curtain to Alice's cubicle, her mum dissolved into tears, drawing Alice towards her for a hug.

"I'm OK, Mum," Alice muttered, fighting back tears herself. She'd never been so glad to see anyone.

"I know," her mum said, pushing Alice's pale hair back from her face, wincing at the bruise that had appeared at her temple. "I got your message as I got off the tube outside Olympia, and then when I couldn't find you, or Finn and no one knew where you were," her voice broke. "I've never been so worried. And I don't know whether to be mad, or so incredibly proud of you." She paused. "Both, I think. *What* were you thinking?"

"I couldn't let anything happen to Secret," Alice said simply. Her mum gave a small smile and Alice knew she understood.

★

Early next morning Alice left the hospital, clutching her mum's arm and a packet of painkillers. The traffic was quiet and there was a smell of coffee on the cold air from a few street vendors. There was only one place Alice wanted to go: straight to the Hyde Park stables. Alice needed to stroke Secret's neck, to feel his silken red mane between her fingers, to reassure herself that he was actually there and that he was OK.

Clare was waiting at the yard when Alice got there, pale-faced and exhausted-looking.

"Alice," she said, sounding distraught. "I'm just so sorry this happened. If we hadn't swapped stables—"

"Then Kite would have been taken instead," Alice finished for her. She didn't blame Clare, or Gareth.

"Yes, you're right," Clare said. "Kite has gone

now, off to his Olympia stable. The *real* transporter picked him up as planned, although who knows what will happen to him now. Poor chap. Anyway, Secret's OK," she continued. "He came back, had a small feed and a hay net and we kept an eye on him all night. But…"

Alice looked up sharply, hearing the hesitation in Clare's voice. "What?" she said in a worried voice, and Clare frowned.

"He's not injured. We had a vet look over him," Clare explained. "But he's not the same pony who arrived a few days ago. It's like he's lost his sparkle; he's very subdued. He was happy to see Kite but…" Her words hung in the air as Alice headed straight over to Secret.

Secret was standing at the back of his stable. He'd clearly had a good groom and he was wearing his Olympia qualifier rug. His head was lowered, but hearing Alice's footsteps and voice he moved forward, resting his head against Alice's arm and sighing. There were none of the usual kicks of the door or throwing his rubber feed bucket at her. Instead, as Alice rested her own cheek against his forehead, they remained perfectly still.

"Al?" her mum interrupted her gently a few minutes later. "We've got to get Secret over to Olympia by lunchtime at the latest to sign him in, if you are feeling up to it. But I know the police want to talk to you first."

Alice nodded, giving Secret a final stroke. Clare was right, there *was* something different about him.

"I don't know, Mum," she said. "I sort of want to go home."

Her mum looked thoughtful for a minute.

"Let's think about it," she said gently. "You've both been working so hard this year, and remember how excited you were before last night." She paused. "Perhaps if we just take him over there and you can see how he feels during a warm-up?"

Alice hesitated. "OK," she agreed, knowing they could still be home by tonight if she chose.

From then on it was a whirlwind of activity. Rosie and Edward, the two officers from the mounted police unit stopped by.

"How are you doing, Alice?" Rosie smiled kindly, and Alice nodded.

"OK," she said, only half truthfully. Physically she was feeling surprisingly OK, but she and Secret had been through the worst night ever. That was going to take longer to get over than the bruise on her head.

"We'll need to take an official statement at some point," Edward continued. "But we wanted to check in on you. That was some quick thinking last night. If we hadn't got your message, there's no way we would have known where to go."

"What was actually going on?" Alice said.

Rosie looked grim. "We've had suspicions about Nick for years, even in his early showjumping days," she explained. "When The Talisman was put down, a huge insurance payout was made for his loss." She paused. "Only The Talisman didn't die after all."

Alice felt the shock of the words run through her, thinking about Devon, who had mourned the loss of her pony for years.

"We know from files and paperwork found at the depot last night that Nick sold him on the Continent with false papers," Edward explained. "So effectively he profited from his 'loss' twice."

"So that was where Kite was headed?" Alice asked, and Edward nodded.

"Yes, along with two other ponies," he said. "We believe Nick was part of a much wider ring, including a vet who was struck off for misconduct.

That's how he was able to forge the insurance payout. With the value of the ponies who were loaded on to the horsebox last night – along with Kite, if he'd been there – we're looking at fraud in the region of a quarter of a million." He paused, and Alice's mouth fell open. "So a fairly low-priority case – a pony going missing – suddenly becomes something much bigger. We think Kite was booked to go last minute, but he'd probably have ended up there at some point given that he'd recently had a valuation done. We found a whole stack of paperwork relating to him."

Alice remembered Leah's concerns during the lead-up to Olympia, sensing something wasn't right. The vet who had seen Kite must have been part of the circle. And when Leah said Kite wasn't ready to compete at Olympia, Nick fast-tracked his plan.

"And Secret?" she said hesitantly. "What would

have happened to him?"

Rosie and Edward exchanged glances.

"Well," Rosie said. "I'm not sure Nick would have returned your pony. He would have got rid of him, one way or the other."

Alice shuddered.

"I can tell it's all a lot to take in," Rosie continued gently. "But we just wanted to make sure you and Secret were OK, and let you know that the investigation is very much ongoing."

Alice thought of Leah and Devon, super-talented young riders who had been given what they'd thought was an opportunity of a lifetime. But all they'd done was build up the ponies' value so Nick could sell them on in the cruellest way possible. The girl who'd approached Nick on the stand the day before had truly had a lucky escape.

"Anyway, Alice, we'll be in touch. All the best at

Olympia," Edward said, his blue eyes twinkling, and, with a start, Alice was brought back to the present. *Olympia*. The word that had dominated most conversations for the latter part of the year, the thing she'd dreamed about, worked towards … and now it just seemed so insignificant. But her mum was right, she needed to at least take Secret over there, and see how he went. Trying to smile, she nodded.

"Thanks," she said, with a lot more conviction than she felt.

Chapter 15

Alice was thoughtful later as she got Secret ready to load him up for the journey across London. He was so quiet. It had to be psychological, Alice concluded, remembering the fear in his eyes the previous night.

"Come on, boy." She placed her arms around him. "I'm not going to leave your side. *Ever*."

As they loaded him on to the box, Secret

hesitated, and Alice felt his tension. He normally bounded up the ramp, keen for another adventure. Had he put up a fight the previous evening, she wondered, when he realised he wasn't with her, when he realised it was all wrong? Had they hurt him? Alice felt her anger bubble up.

Alice's mum crawled along with the London traffic in the lorry once Secret was on board, and Alice stared at the vast expanse of green park, where she'd been so excited to ride. And the days she'd had in London *had* been magical: the hacks around the park, the ice skating, and watching Olympia from backstage. But it all felt like a lifetime ago now.

★

"Alice!"

A familiar voice met Alice as she walked Secret into the stabling area backstage at Olympia, and, rushing forward, Leah gave Alice a hug.

"Hi," Alice muttered, feeling a little overwhelmed, clutching Secret's lead rope for dear life. "How's Kite? Is he here? Is he safe?"

Leah nodded.

"Yes," she said. "He's safe here for now. He didn't have anywhere to go. Nick had cancelled his livery back home, it seems. But with everything going on … I'm not even sure who he belongs to!" She scuffed her feet on the sand, her green eyes filling with tears. "Turns out Nick was getting sick of us. Kite wasn't getting to the top as quickly as he wanted. Me wanting to withdraw from the class was the last straw. He was just going to get rid of him, move on to the next pony."

Alice's heart went out to her. Kite was still here, but with Leah's sponsorship deal having crumbled, no one was a winner.

"Oh, Leah," Alice started gently, but Leah put her hand up, smiling bravely.

"Hey," she said. "It's OK. He's safe, that's the main thing. And so is Secret."

Alice put her hand on Secret's neck as she and Leah walked towards Secret's allocated stable. Secret was safe, that was true, but Alice still wasn't sure if she wanted to jump. Even the sight of the big jumps backstage hadn't perked him up. Instead he'd just nuzzled into Alice and sighed.

"Is he OK?" Leah asked as Alice put Secret into the temporary stable, just two down from Finn. Someone – Finn probably – had put tinsel round the door, and Alice gave a small smile. Turning to Leah as she slipped Secret's head collar off, she frowned.

"I don't know," she said hesitantly. "The vet said he was fine, but…" She searched for the right words. "It's like for the first time ever, he was terrified. I think when I got taken away by the ambulance, he panicked. He'd 'lost' me again. I've never seen him like that before."

Then she paused. "Actually, I'm thinking of withdrawing him altogether."

Leah bit her lip.

"Oh, Alice, you can't," she said sadly. "You can't let Nick win. Think how hard you've worked, and you've told me how Secret just adores his jumping."

"He does," Alice agreed. "I'm going to ride in the warm-up and then decide from there."

And then, like a piece of home, Finn approached. Without saying anything, he drew Alice in for a hug, and she collapsed against him, as if reassuring herself, that like Secret, he was there, and safe.

"Alice," he said softly. "I'm so glad you're OK. When you fell, and we didn't know how seriously you'd been hurt…" His voice trailed off.

"But now I'm here." She tried to smile.

"Yeah." Finn ran his hand through his dark hair.

"Now you're here."

Then he looked closely at Alice.

"Do you want to be, though?" he asked, and Alice dropped her gaze.

"I'm not sure yet," she said quietly. "It just doesn't seem to matter any more, after last night."

Finn looked thoughtful. "Secret is fine, physically. He really is," he said. "But he was searching for you after you were taken to hospital. I think he was as scared of losing you as you were of losing him."

Alice blinked back tears. "So what shall I do?" she said in a wobbly voice, and Finn put an arm around her.

"You and him are like the other half of each other," he said. "He needs to know everything is OK. He needs you to guide him."

★

Alice tried to hold on to Finn's words later as

she tacked up Secret for their warm-up session. The stable area was full of the excited chatter of the other pony club members who'd qualified for the Christmas Tree Stakes the next day, but Alice was still deep in thought as she smoothed down Secret's saddle pad, which had been bought especially for Olympia, a gorgeous white one with gold stars.

Zipping her jacket up and pulling on her gloves, she swung herself lightly into the saddle, waiting for the first flutters of excitement. She frowned. Normally by now Secret would have been bouncing with his eagerness to get into the warm-up arena. He adored the warm-up: all the different ponies going around, the chatter from the riders and the excitement of them flying over the jumps as Alice waited her turn. But instead, he just walked on calmly, hardly seeming to notice the atmosphere. It was like he'd shut down.

Alice's mum, Leah and Finn had gathered to watch as Alice trotted Secret on both reins, before nudging him into his rocking horse canter. With a gap in the crowd, Alice then aimed Secret towards the first warm-up jump, a simple cross pole. He'd been at his very best just before they'd come to Olympia in Alice's last lesson with Angus, and she tried to recall that feeling as Secret cantered into the jump. But all she could remember was the fear she'd felt that previous night, and suddenly, as a bang echoed from the catering area, she flinched, imagining Nick or one of his associates running towards her ready to grab Secret away. Feeling her tension, Secret hesitated, and then ground to a halt as Alice tried to steady her breathing.

"I'm sorry, boy," she whispered, knowing it was entirely her fault. As boisterous as Secret could be, he was incredibly sensitive to Alice's moods. She knew she had to snap out of it; they were both safe.

Aware of some glances from the other pony club competitors who were circling the arena, Alice took a deep breath. She could see the anxiety all over her mum's face as she turned back into the jump again, this time managing to clear it, holding on to a handful of red mane with shaky hands. But it didn't feel right.

Finn raised the jump, placing one pole behind it to turn the cross pole into a spread, and gave Alice a questioning look.

"OK?" he said carefully, and Alice just nodded, afraid that if she tried to explain herself she might fall apart completely. All she knew was that everything felt wrong.

The jump was bigger now, and Alice knew she really needed to ride it properly. Giving Secret a nudge, she turned the corner in a smooth canter, fixing her eyes on the poles.

Think positive. She tried to remind herself of

Angus's words. *Sit up, sit quietly* ... and then something caught her eye. The bright scarlet of a Hadley Feeds banner – and suddenly Nick's face as he'd driven towards her in the lorry swam in front of her mind. Secret, who'd been cantering into the jump checked again and took off awkwardly, catching the back rail with his hooves and sending it tumbling to the ground. Alice only just managed to cling on, falling awkwardly on Secret's shoulder. There was absolutely no mistaking the looks from the other competitors now. Alice must have looked as though she'd never jumped Secret before. This time she couldn't hold back the tears, hot splashy ones that dripped down on to Secret's mane and the front of the saddle as she rode back towards her mum.

"I can't do it," she sniffed. And then when Leah started to protest, Alice shook her head. "I know," she said. "I know you said if I pulled out Nick had won, but I can't. How can I jump him tomorrow?"

She dropped her reins, and Secret's head hung low.

"It's all wrong, I just want to go home," Alice finished, and her mum nodded.

"It's OK," she said gently. "You gave it a try. I can see your heart isn't in it."

Chapter 16

Finn tried to talk Alice round but it didn't work.

"OK," Finn sighed when he'd realised he wasn't going to get anywhere. "Perhaps you and Secret just need to have a break over the New Year."

Alice nodded, too tired to think any more. They still had to pack up Secret's things and officially withdraw from the class, but all she could focus on was getting home.

"Alice, hi!"

Secret pricked his ears forward as a familiar face appeared over his stable door, along with two others. It was Devon, flanked by police officers Hill and Fairbanks, or Edward and Rosie.

"Alice, I'm so glad you're both OK." Devon let herself into the stable and gave both Alice and Secret a hug. She looked tired, and Alice realised she'd only just found out what had actually happened to her beloved pony Tally. The whole, painful truth.

"Thanks for your help last night," Alice mumbled.

Devon smiled bravely. "I only helped a bit," she said. "But I'm so glad it stopped more ponies disappearing like Tally did."

"Is there any way you could find Tally, now you know…?" Alice asked, but she knew the answer, deep down.

Devon bit her lip. "No," she said, glancing at Rosie, who nodded. "It would be impossible. Sold with false papers and somewhere in Europe, he'll be untraceable, exactly as Nick wanted. Anyway." She paused and her eyes glistened with tears. "I just know he's gone, you know? I don't mean sold. I mean, he's gone. I just … know."

For a few moments the girls were silent, reflecting on this, and Alice tried not to let herself think about Secret disappearing like Tally had.

Then Devon seemed to shake herself and glanced at Alice's partly packed tack trunk in the corner of the stable.

"What's going on?" Devon asked. "Your class is tomorrow, right?"

"It is," Alice replied quietly. "But I'm going to withdraw Secret. He doesn't feel right, after everything…"

Devon looked as though she was just about to

say something when Rosie interrupted.

"We were hoping you might stay this evening though," she smiled. "The press has got wind of the story, and we thought it might make the demonstration tonight extra special if we brought Secret in. He's the hero of the hour, helping to save those ponies!"

"What do you mean?" Alice said in a confused voice.

"We just thought it would be nice if you could lead Secret into the arena at the end, and we'll use the time to explain some of the work the police do," Edward continued. "What do you think?"

Alice thought about this. The stable was booked for the night. It was already growing dark and probably icy outside and would make more sense to all get a good night's sleep and do the journey in the morning. And, she thought, with a little flutter of excitement, they'd get to take part in Olympia after all. Not the jumping as she'd imagined, but at least they could get a nice photo and it would be a good memory after all the bad stuff that had happened. If all she had to do was lead Secret in and stand him still, that would be fine.

"OK," she said with a smile. "I'll ask Mum."

★

It didn't take too long to sort out. Alice's mum, clearly tired from the past twenty-four hours, had been only too happy for Alice and Secret to stay, and Alice could watch another performance of the Rebel Riders as well. With Kite's future still looking uncertain, he was also staying the night. Alice could tell Leah was devastated by the thought of losing him but was putting on a brave face.

"It's Secret's night," she tried to smile when Alice gently questioned her about it.

"But, Leah," Alice said. "What's going to happen now?"

Leah shook her head. "I don't know," she said. "The pony sponsorship was Nick's thing. I imagine Kite will be put up for sale but I hope I get Christmas with him, perhaps work out if I can do anything. But…" And she paused, swallowing hard. "I don't think I can."

Alice remembered Leah's words, how she would have done things so differently if Kite had been her very own pony, and was even more grateful for Secret.

Alice, the mounted police, Leah and Alice's mum sat on the sidelines and watched Finn's performance. Everyone was hugely impressed, even Alice's mum, who didn't have much time for stunt riding!

"Gosh," she said, glitter confetti raining down to thunderous applause as Finn made his final gallop across the arena behind Celia. "It's a step up from the Flying Fillies, isn't it! I wonder what he'll do after this?"

Alice glanced at her mum and bit her lip. Her mum had a point. Having tasted the high life with the Rebel Riders, and what with Sasha's new job in the Middle East, would Finn want to return to his old life? Then she shook the thought from her head. The past day had been stressful enough without adding *that* to the equation! Instead she joined in the cheering, feeling her tummy flip over as Finn galloped past and smiled right at her.

Alice thought about the days she used to hang out at the ringside, watching Finn ride at shows with his sister, wondering who he was and if he'd ever notice her. They'd all come so far since then: her, Finn *and* Secret.

Secret. She had about half an hour before the police horse demonstration. The plan was that

Edward would explain who Secret was and what had happened, then Alice would lead her pony in to the arena. The little red gelding was already groomed and gleaming, and Alice had quickly polished her bridle in anticipation. Peeling herself away from the arena side she wandered over to his stable, waving at Rosie and Edward as they walked their beautiful big horses around the warm-up area.

A huge applause met the mounted police as they rode down the famous tunnel and into the international arena. Alice knew from the last few days that the demonstration was extremely popular, and the crowd was even bigger tonight. Hearing the now-familiar music start to play, a shiver went down Alice's spine as she clutched Secret's reins near the entrance, thinking once again how the police cars had screeched to a halt outside the gates of the industrial estate. As if reading her thoughts, Secret nuzzled against her as they watched the demonstration.

"Good luck, Alice!" Devon appeared next to her in breeches, ready for her evening class. All of a sudden, as the police horses lined up for a final time, there was a burst of applause.

"We wanted to tell you about something that happened here in London, last night…" And Alice heard Edward's voice start to tell their story to the crowd. Hearing the words spoken out loud made her realise once again just how brave Secret had been.

"So please, put your hands together and thank a very courageous little pony and his very brave owner!" Edward then said, and Alice started to lead Secret down towards the arena where Edward was addressing the audience, the rest of the mounted police standing in a semicircle around him. As the spotlight fell on her and Secret, she was suddenly aware of thousands of pairs of eyes on them.

Then the clapping started, quiet at first then louder and louder until the whole audience were on their feet and the roar was almost deafening. For the first time all day, Secret pricked up his ears and Alice saw the light coming back into his eyes as he gazed around him. Smiling, Edward approached on horseback, and it was as if Secret recognised the horse Edward was riding from his escape in Hyde Park. Craning his neck forward, Secret reached up to nuzzle the big bay.

"May I?" Edward gestured forward to take Secret's reins and Alice handed them over. Rosie came to ride beside him and Secret, used to Alice's mum leading him all over the lanes behind Ella, bounded forward before Alice could stop him.

"I think he wants a lap of honour," Rosie grinned. "Can we?"

"OK!"

Alice stood back as the rest of the mounted police rode up behind Rosie and Edward, and then to the delight of the crowd they trotted smartly around the huge arena. Secret, so small and slight in between the two huge police horses pushed into his trademark extended trot, meaning the two big bays were having to keep up with him rather than the other way round. The crowd went wild, drumming their feet and clapping with delight as Secret further exaggerated his trot, his red mane flying and his little curved ears pricked forward as far as they could.

To the cheers of the crowd, the police horses and Secret completed another two laps of the arena as Alice stood proudly, blinking back tears. She'd been so caught up in the worry and stress of the past twenty-four hours that it hadn't really sunk in just how much of a hero Secret was. Thanks to him, three ponies were safe. Secret had been in the wrong place at the wrong time, but he'd managed to save the day.

"What a boy!" Edward grinned as they came to a stop by Alice, and, taking back the reins, she saw the change in her pony. Buoyed up by the excitement of the crowd, Secret looked as though he wanted to do it all again, but instead he nudged Alice hard, and she placed her arms around him, before leading him out to more thunderous applause. As they walked, or rather jogged, back down the tunnel to the stabling and warm-up area, it was as though the tension was draining away.

Finn met her at the end of the tunnel.

"That was amazing," he grinned. "The crowd *loved* him!"

"I know." Alice patted the little red gelding again and again. "And look, he's almost back to his old self!"

It was true. It was as though Secret had just jumped the most amazing clear round at a big show and was playing up to the audience, but at the same time checking in with Alice as he nudged her over and over, his eyes shining, dancing slightly from hoof to hoof.

"He obviously just needed a bit of adoration from the crowd," she grinned.

Finn looked thoughtful. "Actually, I think he's realised he's OK; he's back with you," he said gently.

Alice thought about this, then had an idea. "I cut my warm-up slot earlier," she said slowly. "I wonder if there's any way I can have a jump now, while it's free? Just so I can end things on a good note..."

Finn nodded. "Let's ask."

★

In the end it was Devon who managed to persuade the stewards to allow Alice to finish her warm-up session.

"I'll make sure she's OK." Devon smiled at the man who oversaw the warm-up ring, but his eyes were already twinkling.

"Is this the pony that helped the police?" he said warmly. "How can I say no! Fifteen minutes then, no more."

And so Alice was in the surreal position of cantering around as famous showjumpers warmed up around her, a Whitaker here, a Skelton there. It seemed as though word had got round the stables about Secret's heroics, and everyone wanted to chat to Alice and congratulate the little red pony, who basked in the praise.

"If he hadn't already got his mojo back with the police," Finn had chuckled, "I'd say all this attention was definitely helping him!"

Secret's restored confidence also lifted Alice. The jumps were much smaller than the ones the big showjumpers were soaring over, but to Alice and Secret they were enormous. Alice swallowed hard, reminding herself they were no different to the jumps she flew over in her lessons with Angus.

Nudging him into a canter she could immediately feel the difference in her pony. He wanted to jump, and so did Alice. Together they were strong; they were a team. Alice couldn't help but laugh with delight, feeling Secret lift and soar over the coloured poles, his neat hooves tucked into his body, no danger of any poles being touched. It was effortless. Landing softly in the sand, Secret gave a small buck of joy, and when Alice brought him to a halt, he turned round, gently mouthing her boots. It was a habit he'd had since he was very young, and Alice had never tried to deter him. It was Secret, and he was back.

All of a sudden she was starting to regret her decision of withdrawing from the class.

"It's almost a shame I pulled out," she said, thinking out loud, but knowing the decision had been right at the time for Secret. "He's never felt better!"

But Alice's mum cleared her throat. "Actually," she said, and everyone turned to look at her. "I never officially withdrew you from the class. I was on my way over to do so, but then got distracted by the mounted police."

"So … I can still jump tomorrow?" Alice felt as if she'd been thrown a lifeline, and her mum nodded, a smile breaking.

"Yes, it would seem so."

Alice looked at Finn, who gave her the thumbs-up, and then placed her arms around Secret's neck. It didn't matter if they won or lost. Secret was happiest with her, jumping courses, and she was happiest with him. And tomorrow afternoon, whatever the result, she'd get to load Secret into their lorry and take him home. Her mind was made up.

"Let's do it!"

Chapter 17

Despite her exhaustion, Alice tossed and turned that night in her hotel bed, unable to sleep. She still hadn't got used to the sounds of traffic and the lights, which whirled around on her ceiling every now and again as another ambulance whizzed past. She felt as though she'd experienced every emotion under the sun recently, from fear, to anger, to sadness, to pride and determination.

Earlier that evening she hadn't wanted to leave Secret in his stable, the horror of finding him gone still too fresh in her mind, but after a chat with the security guards on site, she'd felt a little better. They had the likes of Valegro, the world-famous Olympic dressage horse to look after, and Secret would be just as carefully guarded. But even so, she'd kept running back to the little gelding for one last hug.

Alice had been painfully aware of Leah in the stable opposite her, her arms around Kite, tears streaming down her face as she buried her head in Kite's conker-and-white mane. Alice's heart went out to the other girl. She wished there was something she could do. Inviting Leah down to ride at her house occasionally seemed pointless. Leah was an incredibly talented rider and now her future had been ripped away. All Alice knew was that when she trotted into that huge international arena tomorrow, she was going to jump for both herself *and* Leah.

★

There had been little point in setting an alarm. Alice had been awake long before it had been due to go off, thinking about the day ahead. It had been too early for breakfast at the hotel, but Alice knew she wouldn't have been able to eat it anyway.

As they strolled towards Olympia and the huge signs for the show loomed into view, she pulled her coat up around her face and gave a shiver, partly from cold and partly from nerves, and tried to quell a wave of nausea. For a second she wondered if she was doing the right thing. They *could* be loading up and heading home. Then she shook herself, thinking of the pure joy in Secret's expression as he completed a lap of honour with the mounted police, and the way he'd soared over the practice jumps during their second warm-up.

There was already a buzz of activity in the stables as Alice arrived. Grooms mucked out the top showjumpers' horses and smiled at Alice, wishing her good luck as she grabbed her fork and set to work on her own stable. It was the biggest relief to see Secret happily munching hay.

"Hey." A familiar voice made Alice look up and smile. It was Finn, wearing a grey hooded top, his black hair tousled and unkempt. Alice was so used to seeing Finn in his elaborate costumes for his displays that when he dressed like a normal teenager it took her by surprise.

"Breakfast?" Finn continued, stifling a huge yawn.

Alice shook her head. "Nope," she grimaced. "I'll be sick."

"After your class then." Finn grinned and then

looked up and waved. "Dad!" he called. "Over here."

And with Angus present, and Alice's mum starting to fuss around Secret, combing out his mane for the hundredth time, Alice tried to pretend they were just at Hilltops, ready for a local showjumping class. She was a bundle of nerves, but full of excitement too. Then, looking over the aisle at Kite, who stood calmly resting a leg, letting the atmosphere wash over him, she felt a wave of sadness.

★

Her earlier excitement was quickly replaced by only nerves when Alice walked the course later. It wasn't just that the jumps were higher and more technical than anything she had jumped before. It was everything else!

The atmosphere in the huge arena was electric as the grand doors opened and the crowds began to spill in. Very soon the stands would be completely full and Secret would have to contend with the lights and the cheers and the distraction of people getting up and down, and the camera crews. Alice knew from riding her mum's ponies on show days that the atmosphere could unsettle even the quietest of ponies.

As Alice planned her course with Angus, discussing where Secret's strengths would come into play, the excitement slowly started to creep back. Even more so when she started to tack up Secret, smoothing down his new saddle cloth and tightening the noseband on his simple snaffle, which had been oiled and polished the night before in her hotel room. Secret seemed to mirror her happiness, his eyes bright and shiny as he reached over to every passing person, hoping for a pat. However, Alice's excitement faded with the sight of Leah's tear-stained face as she fled the stable area.

"Leah!" Alice frowned, giving Secret a pat as she slipped his head collar over his bridle. She had to be warming up in less than two minutes but she needed to check her friend was OK.

"Leah, what's up?"

Catching up with the other girl, Alice pulled her hand gently back as Leah spun round, her face anguished.

"Oh, Alice." Leah collapsed in her arms, her voice heavy with pain. "I didn't want to see you before the class. I didn't want to put you off."

"What is it?" Alice steered her friend out of the way of a big horse approaching the warm-up.

"It's Kite," Leah managed between sobs. "He's been sold. I'll never see him again!"

"Oh, Leah, I'm sorry."

Alice gave her a friend a hug. But as hard as it was, she needed to push Leah's pain out of her mind for the next hour. She had to concentrate on the class ahead, the class she'd been practising for since summer. But now she had a renewed determination to jump for both herself and Leah, to show Nick that he hadn't completely won. Even though he was in a police cell, he'd still managed to crush poor Leah's dreams. Nudging Secret towards the practice fence a short while later, she felt her heart lift with his feet as he sailed over. They could do this, she thought. They had to do this.

It was almost an out-of-body experience as Alice trotted Secret down the famous tunnel towards the international arena. As it opened up in front of them, it seemed to grow in size, stretching out for miles and miles, the jumps looming above Alice like tower blocks. There was a round of applause as Alice rode in, and, glancing up, her eyes were drawn to a huge banner where her friends from

Hilltops were sitting. *Go Alice and Secret!* the words read, and she smiled, briefly reminiscing about how far they'd come since the first few lessons at Hilltops when she thought she'd never be able to control her red gelding! As the electronic bell sounded, the vast stands fell silent. Alice's heart was beating so loudly, she was convinced everyone could hear it.

Dry-mouthed, she steadied Secret into a springy trot, before nudging him back into his trademark rocking horse canter. It had been something Angus had taught her, to make use of every second before they had to cross the electronic line instead of rushing to start. She had to get Secret listening to her, to focus his energy and enthusiasm. Circling once, she felt a surge of adrenalin as Secret locked on to the first fence. Then the enormous crowds melted away, and it was just Alice and her red pony.

For the next minute and a half it was as though the past week had never happened and she was back in the arena at Hilltops, Angus smiling encouragement as she and Secret cleared fence after fence.

A big oxer to start, and on to the double, painted like brightly coloured candy canes. A perfect stride between the two fences and over the second, turning like a minnow in mid-air as Alice used Secret's excellent agility to his advantage, cutting precious seconds off their time as he cut the corners like a barrel racer, never losing his rhythm, each jump taken with precision timing. Over the upright, the one with the Christmas tree fillers that had caused problems for earlier competitors as their ponies spooked at the decorations, but not Secret. Flicking one red ear back and forth, listening to Alice all the time, he leapt over the fence, joy radiating through his body as he cantered on to the next.

The big triple spread, the bounce, the hanging gate, they all disappeared under Secret's flying hooves as Alice laughed with delight. And to think she wasn't going to jump! But she knew Secret so well: if he'd lost confidence then there was no way he'd be able to clear the fences like he was doing now. It had taken the crowd, and being with Alice, to put the spring back into his step.

Alice could sense the collective breath of the audience being held as she made a daringly tight turn down towards the last two fences, the last double. Had it been *too* daring? It left Secret barely two strides to jump, but as if one with Alice, the little red pony made the most tremendous effort and cleared the fence, landing and taking one perfect stride before the very last jump on the Olympia course disappeared under his flying hooves. All of a sudden the arena had become blurry as Alice's vision was clouded by tears. The roar from the crowds grew as the commentator announced their time, which put them firmly in the lead, and Alice reached down as Secret slowed to a trot, hugging him over and over.

Chapter 18

"Amazing, amazing!"

There was quite a crowd of people waiting backstage for Alice, all patting Secret and hugging her at the same time. Alice's mum was crying and hugging Alice's dad, who'd managed to make it just before Alice went on. Angus was grinning from ear to ear, pride all over his face. Celia and the Rebel Riders led a chorus of applause as Rosie and Edward clapped her heartily on the back.

"Bravo, young lady!" Edward smiled, and Alice blushed.

"Thanks to you and the rest of the mounted police last night," she said, knowing it had helped Secret get his confidence back, and Edward nodded.

"The least we could do," he said happily. "Your pony's quite the hero!"

Devon gave her a cheer as she walked back to the stables, but there was no sign of Leah. Alice thought perhaps it was too painful for her. However, everything melted away when she saw the one face she'd been searching for: Finn. And just like at the summer championships when she'd leapt off Secret and he'd hugged her so tightly, he did the same again, and Alice felt nothing but contentment. It was her, Secret and Finn, and now they could go home.

★

In the end, no one could come near Alice's time. They were the fastest by over three seconds. There was a huge cheer as the last rider finished, a red-haired boy on a lovely bay who congratulated Alice backstage where she was walking Secret round and round.

"Congratulations," he grinned. "I tried, couldn't do it. Your pony is something else. You're totally going to be the new pony club hero now!"

Alice remembered the days of coaxing Secret into the show ring, how he'd hated it so, and how she'd had to really convince her mum to let her go to the jumping lessons at pony club. *Everything* had been worth it, for this moment. A steward brought over her gorgeous winner's rug, and, fastening it over the saddle, Alice swung herself back up, ready to go back into the huge arena for the best lap of honour of her life. But something was niggling away at her.

As Secret stood proudly between the two Christmas trees, the spotlight beaming down on him as a lady in a sparkly black dress handed Alice a huge trophy, the commentator stood next to them and gave Secret a pat.

"Wonderfully ridden, young lady," he smiled, before turning to the audience. "For those who weren't here last night," he continued, "you might not realise that this pair have been very brave recently…"

And as he recounted Secret's tale, Alice felt tears prick her eyes. When the commentator handed her the microphone, she knew she had to say something.

"Um…" She hesitated, her voice sounding years younger as it resounded around the arena. "I just wanted to say…" She swallowed hard. "There was another pony entered for this class, a pony who has someone who loves him just as much as I love Secret." She held the trophy up. "This is for you too, Leah and Kite."

The audience erupted into applause. Alice wasn't even sure if Leah was still at Olympia. She wouldn't have blamed her if she'd already gone home. But she'd meant every word, even if Leah couldn't hear them. Seeing how Leah had had her future taken away had only made Alice appreciate Secret more, if that was possible. They'd won the biggest class of their career so far and they had so much more to give. But as Alice cantered round, waving at the crowds, delighting in Secret's joy at showing off in front of such a huge audience, she knew that for now, she wanted to get home and reflect on what had happened.

★

"I came to say goodbye."

Alice gave a start as she untacked Secret back

in the temporary stable, once all the well-wishers had disappeared. She'd fully expected Leah to be long gone by now.

"You were amazing," Leah continued. "I'm sorry I didn't stay backstage with everyone. It was just too hard."

"It's OK." Alice gave her friend a hug. "What's going to happen now?"

Leah shook her head. "I'll go home," she said quietly. "Tomorrow will be the first day in years I don't have to get up to muck out a pony. I guess I'll be OK, I'll have to find something else to do. I just don't know what."

"Actually." A friendly voice made them both jump and Devon Jenkins leaned on the stable door along with a lady Alice didn't recognise. "That might not be necessary."

"Jackie!" Leah gave a gasp, and the lady with Devon smiled. Alice realised this must be the lady who'd taught her to ride, the one Leah had talked about on their hack through the park.

"Hello, Leah."

"Now, if you want to come with me," Devon grinned at Leah, "I think you might find you have a stable to muck out after all."

Exchanging glances, Alice followed Leah out of the stable, giving Secret a pat.

"Back in a minute, boy."

In Devon's stable a familiar conker and white head popped over the door on the other side, giving a deep, rumbling whicker.

"Kite!" Running forward, Leah hugged the pony, burying her face in his mane before turning to Devon, her face wet with tears.

"I … I don't understand!" she stammered, and Devon smiled.

"He's yours," she explained gently. "When I found out what had happened, I knew it was too late for Tally." She held up her silver bracelet and touched the little horse head, her eyes full of sadness. "But I could honour him by buying Kite, securing his future." Her voice cracked with emotion. "You remind me of myself. And someone needed to give you that chance."

Leah was too overcome to speak, but tears continued to stream down her face as she clung to Devon and to Kite. Alice wiped her eyes as well, the emotion of the moment overwhelming.

"I've arranged it all with Jackie," Devon continued with a smile. "She told me how you loved helping at the yard before Nick came along. Kite can live there if you're happy to help out there again."

"We've all missed you," Jackie said. "I won't be able to do the big shows, but we can go back to local stuff, all those things you enjoyed before."

Leah nodded. "I'd love that. I've missed you

all so much." Then she turned to Alice. "I can't believe it! Isn't this amazing?"

Alice nodded. They were both getting to take their beloved ponies home after all.

"It is," she agreed in a choked voice. "It's a miracle. A Christmas miracle!"

★

"Are you sure you want me to wear this?" Finn said, sounding grumpy, but he was grinning as well.

"Yes." Alice giggled, reaching up to arrange the toy antlers she'd clipped on to Finn's skullcap. "It's tradition – we always used to have a Christmas Eve fancy-dress ride."

"OK." Finn mock-rolled his eyes. "For you … I'll do it." And he smiled at Alice with such warmth that despite the freezing temperatures, she felt warm inside.

Turning back to Secret, she gave her little pony

a hug. He'd been welcomed back home just a few days ago with a hero's reception and had adored every second, going from stable to stable to nudge all his friends. Alice wondered if he was doing it partly to reassure himself he was home and safe.

She'd gone all-out on his Christmas Eve outfit, and he was wearing a special red exercise rug trimmed with a furry white border, matching bandages and antlers attached to his bridle. Alice had always ridden out on Christmas Eve in festive wear, until the year Honey had been killed. It felt good to pick up the tradition again with Finn by her side.

"So tell me," Finn said, his breath hanging in the cold air as they clattered up the road and towards the village where they were going to circle the green and get a hot chocolate from the café. "What did Devon say?"

"Well," Alice said, thinking back to the amazing

afternoon she'd won the Pony Club Christmas Tree Stakes and Devon had bought Kite for Leah. "She's offered both me and Leah a work-experience spot next year at her yard. We can take our ponies."

"That's cool!" Finn said. Then he looked at Alice closely. "Isn't it?"

Alice nodded, waving at a car whose occupants were smiling delightedly at the sight of the ponies and their riders in festive fancy dress.

"Yes, it's amazing. She'd give us lessons, we can help at shows, we might even get to ride her horses. But..." She tried to think about how she'd felt as they'd returned from Olympia. Mainly exhausted from the whirlwind of emotion that had accompanied their London visit. Putting Secret back in his familiar stable with the nibbled manger, and sinking into her own bed surrounded by posters from years of *Pony* magazine had been the best feeling of all. "I guess I just want to soak everything up, just for a bit."

Finn nodded, as if he understood.

"It's next year," he said. "Just enjoy Christmas first. Actually I—" He paused. "I've been offered something as well. Something that would take me away from here. Celia's offered me a full-time job. Obviously there's loads to sort, school, home, that sort of thing."

Alice was silent for a minute. It had been hard when Finn had been away training, but it had always been temporary. They were always going to be reunited.

"What do you think you'll do?" she asked finally, and Finn paused.

"I think I'm going to go for it," he said, and Alice gave a start, absorbing his words. But to her surprise, it felt OK. She was OK. They were moving in different directions, different worlds, but their one connection – their shared love of ponies – would always draw them together even if they lived far apart. "But first," Finn continued, "I'm just going to enjoy Christmas."

Then as they reached the village green, he turned to Alice and smiled. Even with the ridiculous reindeer antlers, he was still the most handsome boy Alice had ever met.

"Whatever happens, I'll always be there for you, Alice, if you need me."

"Ditto." Alice smiled, placing her arms around Secret. He jigged a bit in the cold air, and the green glittered and sparkled in the weak winter sun, just as the sound of jingle bells spilled out of the village pub as the door opened and some jolly pub-goers burst out into the early afternoon.

Alice smiled happily. She and Secret had been catapulted into the spotlight, both for their jumping success and Secret's part in the dramatics of the Hadley Feeds scandal. *Pony* mag had even put them on the front cover of their Christmas special, and Secret's face was suddenly everywhere.

Winning at Olympia had been a dream come true, and it felt like just the beginning of something truly amazing. But for now, Alice was going to enjoy being at home, hanging out with her beloved red pony. Burying her head in his mane, she smiled.

"Merry Christmas, Secret. And thank you."

Acknowledgements

Thank you to the wonderful team at Nosy Crow, in particular Kirsty and Fiona for all their expert help and guidance and Nic for her amazing design skills and for producing the most beautiful covers. A huge thank you to my lovely editor Sarah who totally 'got' Finn and Alice from the start and has been amazing to work with. And thanks to the whole team at Nosy Crow who support the books so brilliantly from start to finish!

Special thanks to Jolie Darton, former owner of Butler – our beautiful cover star. Jolie made sure Butler looked like a superstar ready for his photo shoot! Good luck in your new home, Butler!

Finally, writing pony books really is the best job in the world and I must thank my husband Clive who supports me every step of the way despite his own very busy job running the family farm. And of course my children Lara, whose love for ponies mirrors my own, and sweet baby Jasper who smiles all day.